Prepare yourself for an unforgettable ride; when ~~retreat, they never expected to be trapped inside (~~ the house's dark secrets, they find themselves facing supernatural and occult challenges, and the lines between reality and horror begin to blur. Lauren Carter's When the Demons Take Hold is a gripping novella that will keep you on the edge of your seat. With its vivid descriptions and intricate plot, this folk horror story will haunt you long after you turn the final page.

Lauren Carter's paranormal novella is a creepy little gem. It lures you in and you think you're in for a traditional English haunted manor noir. You're not. This story of five authors drawn to the remote countryside for a writer's retreat will pull you in with shockingly original horror. I definitely won't be able to sleep tonight. And I'm ok with that. - Heidi Blakeslee, author of *Neurotica*

WHEN THE DEMONS TAKE HOLD is a unique, immersive, and utterly terrifying story. It has strong characters, a distinctive voice for its narrator, and jarring horror sequences that never let you get too comfortable. This book proves that knowing the tropes can't always stop you from falling into them, and sometimes it's far worse to know what will happen. - Cat Voleur, author of *Revenge Arc*

Claustrophobic and unsettling, *When The Demons Take Hold* will have you feeling like you're stuck inside the house along with Sage, April, and the others and you'll be desperate to find the way out before it takes you too. - Samantha Eaton, author of *The Insatiable Hunger of Trees*

Lauren Carter takes the haunted house trope and gives it a unique twist, while also interweaving a multigenerational story of love and loss. It was a solid, quick read, and I enjoyed the unexpected way Carter took the story. Any fan of ghosts, revenge, or just plain old hauntings, this isn't something you want to pass up. - Micah Castle, author of *Reconstructing A Relationship*

Nothing is as it seems: an innocuous retreat turns into something more sinister. Carter carves out a tapestry of terror in this claustrophobic nightmare. - Aquino Loayza, author of *Deep*

Carter presents a fast-paced ride with this tale of a writer's retreat gone wrong. Spend the night, but be careful what you say, as words have a way of catching up with you in this place. Carter's protagonist is sharp, witty, fresh, and funny, and you won't regret spending time with her. Come to Rosemary Hollow looking for a story; in the end, you'll get one. - Holley Cornetto author of *We Haunt These Woods*

When The Demons Take Hold

ALSO BY LAUREN CARTER

Let's All Go to the Lobby

Your Darling Death

When The Demons Take Hold

A Novella by Lauren Carter

abuddhapress@yahoo.com

ISBN: 9798386456542

Alien Buddha Press 2023

©™®

Lauren Carter 2023

Cover design by: Christy Aldridge (Grim Poppy Design)

Inside artwork by: Natacha and Afkar

The following is a work of fiction. Any similarities to actual people, places, or events, unless deliberately expressed otherwise by the author are purely coincidental.

For Barney,

who didn't contribute anything to this,

but is a gorgeous lil man.

Chapter 1

I will do anything for a story.

Even if it means spending three days with a bunch of strangers in the middle of nowhere.

I've never considered a writer's retreat before but, then again, I've never been stuck before. They're always advertised as a quiet space to work in – free from distractions. I have been blaming the city noise for my lack of imagination. Which makes complete sense, right?

Even the littlest of things used to trigger an idea, but I don't even have the start of one.

I Googled and clicked through several (expensive) retreats which mostly resembled cults. Some even had house rules which told you what and when to eat and had specific times of day for breaks. One even went to the extent of being mostly outdoors, strictly pencil and paper.

I swear I could see a yellow hut in the background of one of the photos.

I went deeper into the web, and by deeper, I mean going past the first page of Google, and came across April Young's blog. I recognised her immediately as she's the author of the *Ever a Never After* series – a famous romance/contemporary series which is fifteen books strong. It's about two women and their lives together – growing up, getting married, and everything in between that. I believe the characters are in their sixties now in the last book published.

Romance is not my sort of thing at all (hence the lack of it in my life) but it's a bestseller in a lot of countries and has been optioned for a film series (and I may have read one or two of them despite lack of interest). Throw in some spooks and I'm in. No offense to contemporary but I already have to deal with the real world in reality, I want to escape it in my books.

She had written a post about finding a newly rebuilt country home and wanted to rent it for her own writing retreat next month for a few days but needed four other people to join her. She already had the other three but needed one last person, so I thought, why not?

After speaking to her back and forth, I deduced she wasn't a killer. I couldn't say for the others though.

Though, I did have suspicions as to why "publishes one or sometimes two books a year" April Young would want to do a writer's retreat when she had expressed this was her first. I did a little digging to find news of her separation from her wife. If she was unhappy about it, she gave nothing away during our calls.

I quickly sorted out plans, even giving my editor some hope (and by editor, I mean my cousin). I could probably hire a qualified one, but my cousin is happy to be paid via early access to the book and a nice meal out now and then. I probably could also be swayed in that way for a good book – not to brag and say my books are good but they seemed to always praise them.

'Send me whatever you have – even the crap parts,' they said, helping me shove all my stuff into my bags.

'Spence, I only ever send you the crap.' I hand them more things to be packed and neatly folded but they soon enough mess it up again by shoving my stuff into one of the bags.

'Oh yes, I forgot,' Spence said. 'I'm the actual brains behind this operation.' They chuckle at their joke while actually breaking my case by slamming themselves on it. 'Oops.'

'Thanks for that.' It's only a crack and it will still work but it's new and it's not like I'm swimming in gold. Spence smiles apologetically and I know it's likely that by the time I get back they will have bought me a new one.

'You know,' they say, quickly changing the subject. 'You could always write about that school – early 1900's I believe plus its sort of close by.' I know exactly what school they are going on about and it's nowhere nearby. Spence seems to think everything that is in Scotland is close by somehow like everything is just down the road.

'I'll think about it.' This means I won't and, even though I've said this many times to Spence, they still smile thinking they've put a great idea into my head.

WHEN THE DEMONS TAKE HOLD

Getting out of the city to the country was difficult, I hadn't even heard of Three Tree Village before, but it was north of Edinburgh, and I had to change trains twice. There isn't even a station of any kind for the village, the nearest is Ardgay, and then a small trek to it. I regret bringing so much stuff with me, but I have notes written down across several expensive, pretty notebooks and devices and I never know which notes I'll need. Not that any of them have anything concrete in them right now.

The wind has really picked up too - I'm getting more irritated by my hair flying in front of my face, I knew I should have worn it up, but it feels too heavy on my head after a while. The problem is every time it flies in front of my face, all I can see is my ginger locks and not what's ahead of me. Not exactly great for a hike. I should have thought about how much colder it would be here than at home and worn a scarf and gloves. At least it's not snowing or rainy – just a normal, gloomy day.

Three Tree Village has a population of less than a hundred. I did my research on it beforehand to not only see where we would be staying, but also to see if it had any interesting history. Turns out, it's so small due to landslides that cut it off from a neighbouring village seventy years ago. One whole village is now two halves and Three Tree got the short end of the stick. There's now a couple of miles between them.

Though that is interesting, it's not what I'm looking for.

The village is made up of stone cobbled roads, with only one car parked on the main road. There's a post office with a small shop inside too and a phone box but the rest is made up of residential housing (according to Wikipedia, which we all know is very reliable). It's almost as if someone took a piece of Edinburgh and dumped it here. I will admit, it does have some beauty to it despite it looking a little bit like run-down *Balamory* with its colourful houses.

I pull out my printed Google map and try to decipher my scribbles when a gruff man, that resembles a bear but is shorter than me, approaches me.

'I doubt you've come to our little neck of the woods on a holiday.' He glances down at my belongings as I swipe the sweat off my forehead. I should have predicted there would be hills. He's got a tweed wool flat cap on, pulled down over his eyebrows – I have no idea how he's supposed to see. He's wearing an oversized body warmer with those types of trousers that have a thousand pockets in them and wellies – which makes sense because of all the mud.

'Not a holiday, a work trip – I guess you could call it.'

'Work trip? Hardly call that sort of thing a trip unless you fell on your way over.' He laughs at his dad joke, to the point where he's almost choking on his own words. After he finishes coughing and sees me not joining in, (but I give him an awkward smile) he continues. 'So, work you say? What work could you be doing around here? Oh!' He snaps his fingers. 'Are you here about our heating? Took you long enough.'

'What?' I say, thinking he's joking but his mouth doesn't move from a thin, pale line across his face. 'I'm a writer–'

'Ah, I should have known. I met one or two of your friends a few hours back. They didn't have as much stuff as you have though.' He looks at all my stuff again, with an eyebrow raised.

'I'm over-prepared, I can't help it. Sorry I don't have the qualifications to help with your heating.' I try walking off at this point, clearly not interested in a conversation with him but albeit thankful for a reason to rest for a minute or two. I've got nothing against him, he's likely harmless but I just want to sit down and consume a lot of food. He's obviously not finished with me though.

He coughs. 'I'll give it another whack and see how that goes but I have bad news for you.'

'Oh?' I stop and wonder what on earth he's going on about. Another landslide took out the country home and I'm a final girl?

'The place you're going, Rosemary Hollow, is another mile trek north of here.'

'A mile!? But Google maps said it was in the village?' I wave the map around and he gestures that he would like to have a glance at it. He mumbles under his breath when looking over it and grabs a pen from his pocket, hovering over the lines with it.

'There are quite a few buildings that belong to Three Tree that aren't in Three Tree,' he says and draws a big circle on the map. 'Rosemary Hollow is the furthest out of the bunch, lucky you.'

'Great,' I say, taking the map back, grabbing my stuff, and preparing my back again. 'Thank you for your help.' I try to mean what

I say but it comes off as sarcastic. It doesn't seem to faze him though as he nods and tips his hat at me.

As I struggle away from him, he calls to me. 'At least the history will make for an interesting story.' He's still not done with me.

'Oh yeah, the landslides.' I don't stop and turn back this time, I know I'm verging on being rude but I'm about to buckle.

'Well, yes, the landslides, of course!' He follows me up the street, giddy with excitement. Whether it's over the story or talking to someone, I'm not sure. I've only seen a few other people and they seem to be minding their own business. 'But I'm talking about Rosemary Hollow.'

'Haunted, is it? Must be with a name like that.' It is what I was hoping for, even if it's just *Casper the friendly ghost* dropping by to say "hey" or just the legend of it. It didn't exactly scream "haunted house" by April's description, but the name is another story.

'By the old family? Maybe, you'll have to tell me. They were complete shut-ins in their last few years, so it is likely to be haunted.' I'll be honest, he's piqued my interest a little – a house full of ghosts or even the rumour of it is intriguing.

I sigh. 'Let me guess, Rosemary was the daughter.'

'Aye, little Rosemary Taylor.' He speaks of her fondly as if he knew her but he couldn't have known her as he's not much older than me. 'You know your history on the place then.'

'No, it's just predictable. She died, then?'

'They all did, didn't they? In the landslides, poor things.' He takes his hat off and holds it to his chest while still walking beside me. 'But other than that, not much known about the place or the people within if I'm honest. You may find a secret or two.'

'I doubt there are any secrets behind it, being newly re-built. All the secrets have probably been swept away with the landslides,' I say, my interest fading away while I hold back my gasps for air.

'Ah, that's the thing. Some things can't be re-built.' He finally stops walking with me now and I carry on, trying to pretend I'm not dying.

'I'll be on the lookout for secrets and ghosts then and report back,' I say as a goodbye of some kind. I'll be back through the village in a couple of days to go home so will likely run into him again. This time,

I think he's going to let me leave without another word but oh no, there's one more thing to be said.

'If you credit me in your book, describe me as handsome and wealthy. Might attract other Scottish lassies to come here and woo me.'

I don't turn back but still, shout a reply so he can hear. 'I don't know your name and why can't you leave here and find some to woo yourself?'

'If you describe me as I ask, they won't need to know my name. It'll be obvious.'

Chapter 2

Thankfully, I don't get turned around too much as I follow the road (if you could call it that), and soon enough it's signposted on a turning down an even more narrow country lane shrouded with trees. The name of the house is even smaller on the sign than the warning of PRIVATE PROPERTY. At least we won't be disturbed. That being said, I just nodded to a couple walking their dog as I didn't have any hands free to wave. I was hoping the dog would come up to me, but they walked by, head down, even though they weren't sniffing the ground. I'm not the dog whisperer I thought I was.

Everything aches and I think I'm close to a heart attack of some kind. Not a good idea for that to happen, unless the NHS has a few tractors in its service. It's not the most accessible place to get to and I wonder if the owner offered drop-off.

When I reach the end of the lane, I see Rosemary Hollow up ahead – with mountains behind it, fields surrounding it, and a large lake east of the house. The house looks so small with the giant monsters behind it, casting a shadow over it with the sun at its peak. The picture April showed me doesn't do it justice. Whoever owns it must be filthy rich to not only own the house but the land around it.

For once, I'm thankful it's winter as if it was summer, my allergies would be going off like crazy with all these crop fields. They're so overgrown that the path leading up to the house has almost disappeared and they seem to be in all different stages of dying. You would think if they couldn't take proper care of the fields, they would sell them for a fortune.

If I read the history right, those mountains are the source of the landslides - it all started here which means the Taylors were the first to be hit. I remind myself that it was seventy years ago and there hasn't been any since. I doubt they would have rebuilt it if it was deemed unsafe still. It's probably horrible to think, but I hope by some miracle that the little girl died before that happened – I cannot imagine the agony of it.

I try to push that thought out of my mind and instead worry about my suitcase shaking from side to side as I drag it up the pathway – keeping in mind the crack Spence made. Once Rosemary Hollow comes more into view, it's clear that not only does the owner not take care of the fields, but also the property itself.

The house almost looks like a barn mixed with a cottage, but it was once a fancy estate. Most of the property is covered with large windows and there's a balcony that wraps around the back side of the property. I was planning on having my morning caffeine and reading my book there, with such a beautiful view. The paintwork, however, is peeling a little and the roof doesn't look too good – there appears to be several different roofing materials used to make it (metal, felt and some wood too). It may have said re-built, but it didn't say what year it was rebuilt.

When I'm finally standing a few metres away from the house, I have to stop for a breath or two – what a workout I've had, I need a whole cake to myself to gain back any kind of energy. I'm not unfit, I'm just not prepared for a hike.

Please give me a good story, I'm begging you, I think.

I see a figure in the window and realise it's April. She runs out to greet me, a big smile on her face. I suddenly feel very undressed as I'm in basic brown loungewear underneath my massive, black parka and yet she is wearing what I would usually wear to a business meeting – a fancy top with a Peter Pan collar and jeans. Yes, I do go all out for the important things, you would be correct in thinking that (you're not thinking that). Also, very glad I opted for wellies, even if they are bright pink with daisies on them.

'Sage! You made it, I thought you got lost!' She pulls me into an awkward hug with a small pat on my back

'Am I late?' We never agreed on a time, we just said morning so I'm here in the afternoon.

'No, no. Just the last here. Come in and let me introduce you to the others.' She's a lot taller than me, at least six feet compare to my five foot three. I've never seen her blonde hair loose; it's always been tied up in a bun every time I video-called her. She has a pencil tucked behind her ear which is covered in piercings (all gold, which matches her rings). She's very muscular, and we've talked in length about how much we can deadlift (she's currently beating me). She's commented a lot on how jealous she is of my curves and I have to agree, my thick thighs are pretty great.

'Oh, before that let me take your phone. No distractions and all. Don't worry, I'm just putting them in a box I found in the kitchen, and you can come grab it at any time. My thinking was you're less likely to use it if it's not just in your pocket.' I give it to her, and she drops it in with the others as we walk by. I peer in and they're all iPhones except one. We'll have to look at our lock screens to determine whose is whose. Mine is artwork someone made from *Midnight Mass* – I'm guessing the others are boring and have family and friends as theirs instead.

It's very open plan on the ground floor – the entrance, the living room (on the left), and the kitchen (on the right) can be seen from the front door. The walls are a light shade of wood (or look like they are, could easily be wallpapered to create that effect), and the floors too to match. Think of a "cabin in the woods" style.

The kitchen looks brand new with modern appliances but wooden cupboards to match the theme of the rest of the house. The French door fridge/freezer does not match anything at all but at least there's plenty of room for food in it. There's a chandelier made from deer horns (fake, apparently – a concern of April's when first renting) hanging in the entryway with a grand, picnic rug underneath and a large wooden staircase directly in front of me, deer figures carved into the railing. Although the outside of the house doesn't look too good, it's clear the owner spent more time on the inside.

'Can't believe this has been newly re-built,' I say, meaning it doesn't look like the outside has been and the inside looks like it hasn't been touched in all these years. 'They decided to keep the vintage look then? For the most part anyway.' I shrug my coat off and April hangs it up for me. I just hope you can't see the sweat running down my back. It takes several attempts to kick my wellies off.

'I believe that was the plan. The old structure was collapsing and has been unliveable since the time of the landslides. It's only just been deemed safe in the last few years. They managed to save the fireplace though.' I'm about to say hello but April stops me. 'Why don't you take your things up and then I'll introduce you. Your room is upstairs, first on the right.' I nod, first taking out my laptop and notebooks to leave down here so the luggage is much lighter. I catch one of them peering at me over the sofa out of the corner of my eye and the face is not too friendly.

After another struggle, I let out a sharp breath once I've dropped my stuff. Move over whoever the world's strongest person is – I'm clearly in the running now. The room is as you imagine – wood everywhere. The bed, the furniture, and everything in between. With matching red bed covers and another rug – like the one downstairs. Despite the owner not being an interior designer (at least, I doubt they are) it still looks nice and will do for a few days' stay.

I decide to snoop around my room – a tip for whenever you are staying somewhere. You'll either end up being horrified or excited by what you find. I pretend I'm on *Four in a Bed*, a great show for those who are watching daytime TV during writing breaks. Thankfully, no hairs or anything gross in the room.

There is no en-suite, but two bathrooms to share between us. I go into the one next to my room (hoping the walls are thick so I don't hear people using it in the night) to freshen up. I half expect a wooden bath but no, thankfully the bathroom is for the most part modern and basic. The mirror, however, does have a wooden frame and when I catch sight of myself in it, I cringe. There's so much sweat in my hair that it's clearly noticeable and my face, which usually stays quite pale, has bright red patches on my cheeks and forehead. Not the greatest first impression and probably why April sent me upstairs.

I use someone else's hair dryer (it has leopard print on it, which is iconic, and I may steal it) to dry off the sweat and a wet flannel to cool my face down. I'm aware of how long I've been up here and worried they're all thinking I'm taking a huge dump. It's better than them thinking I'm changing clothes because you could see the sweat stains on my other clothes. I decide on my forest green dungarees, a giant pocket in the front for snacks with a white shirt (that has a graphic of Wraith from *NOS4A2* on it, but they won't get to appreciate it) and warm, mustard-coloured socks.

It's a look that I clearly rock.

I dry my face and take one last look at myself in the mirror which is when I notice something odd. My reflection has gone still like I'm looking at a portrait of myself. If you could see me, you would think me odd at that moment as I try winking at myself and moving my head and my body in weird positions. But my reflection is stilled, and she is not looking at me no matter how hard I try to get her to.

No, she is looking behind me.

It's unnerving how soulless my eyes appear to be – they're not their usual crispy mint green colour with specks of orange. No, they're dulled – like someone has added grey to them. I look gone, already departed from the world within a blink. I try to follow her gaze, but she just appears to be looking at the back wall of the bathroom where the bath is. I investigate the wall, looking at the tiles and tracing the lines with my finger, even knocking on the wall but nothing seems amiss. I turn back to face myself.

She's looking me in the eye this time.

I take back what I said, now it's unnerving. I wink again and this time, she winks back at me. Not at the same time – there's a delay between each action as I tilt my head and she copies, and I step back and again she copies. I try to turn away again, to get her to stop but when I turn back, she has her back to me.

What's worse is, she doesn't copy me straight away.

I stare at the back of my own head for a minute, maybe more. I don't even know how long I've been in the bathroom. Finally, she moves and this time, she doesn't copy me exactly. I turned back fast; she's turning back slowly. Her back is slightly hunched, her head hanging to one side like her neck has snapped as she swings around. Her face is no longer neutral, she's smiling at me

But not the kind of smile you would want, it's sinister. Her lips stretch too far across her face, my face, that it starts to crack like glass. She grits her teeth and her eyes narrow – I suddenly feel like a meal.

She lunges at me which causes me to jolt back, falling – narrowingly missing the edge of the bath with my head.

'Sage! Sage, are you okay?' I hear April's voice shouting up at me. I scramble up to see where she, I, have gone but when I look in the mirror, it's me – my own reflection and my own eyes back.

'I just fell, tripped over thin air,' I shout down to April and I can hear her laugh at my joke. I check back to the mirror and trace a line down my face. I chalk it up to my active imagination, at least that's what I tell myself as I leave to head downstairs, making a note to avoid any more mirrors.

Chapter 3

They're all sitting in the living room (except April lingering in the hallway for me), laptops on each of their laps except the one. The fire is lit in the stonework fireplace (with space for logs built in either side) with a large, green velvet sofa wrapping around the coffee table and an empty fruit bowl sitting on it. There are also two huge bookcases on both sides of the fireplace, but they are empty for the most part and a huge grandfather clock lingers in the corner. I've already cooled down from the hike and shaking so it won't be long before I say, "screw it" and I'm sitting in the actual fireplace to get warm again.

April puts a hand on my back and guides me into the living room like I'm a new child in her classroom.

'This is Hallie Walker,' April points to the blonde with her MacBook (which sounds like it's dying) sitting on the sofa. She's white and blonde-haired, like April, but she has a pixie cut that, I won't lie, doesn't look professionally done. I am not one to judge, Spence cuts my hair (yes, they're a hairdresser/book editor). But Hallie's cut looks like I did it and I hope I didn't charge her for it. She looks quite young compared to the rest of us, maybe just a few years into her 20s despite the few wrinkles (it's the babyface she has, it's throwing me off). Thankfully, she's not bothered about her looking her best either as she's in sweats (all white, I could never with the way I throw food around). Hallie turns and smiles at me but says nothing.

'And next to her is Jonas Torres.' He grunts at his name but nothing more. He has brown skin, and he looks like a businessman, not a writer with his uniformed haircut and rectangle glasses – not as cool as my giant, round glasses which I do not need to wear all the time but do anyway. He just needs a suit to complete the look he's going for but instead today, he's wearing jeans and a plain, long-sleeved dark green shirt. He's also got a MacBook but the latest model. I think about my crusty Windows laptop in my bag. Nothing wrong with a Windows (it's certainly cheaper than a Mac) and it's only crusty because it has food all in the keyboard. Note: don't eat and type.

'Last but not least, Reece – just Reece he says,' April says, gesturing to the person in the wingback matching green armchair. He doesn't look up, but at least gives me a wave. He's the only one without a laptop, he's instead opted for a notepad and a pencil. Took him more for a lefty rather than a righty, and I'm not sure why. He looks like a surfer with his sandy, blonde hair falling to his shoulders and russet brown skin. I make a note to ask him later if I can plait it. He's acting like it's summer not winter with a short-sleeved white shirt with a blue, robotic hand design on it (I recognise it as the cover of *The Luminous Dead* – great book and good choice in a t-shirt) and shorts...he's in shorts. It takes me a while, but I finally realise who Reece is.

'You're the author of *Pluto Retaliating*,' I say, and this makes them all pay attention to me, particularly Reece who puts down his writing supplies. It only gets Jonas to glance at me, however.

'Yeah, that's me,' he says, his face turning slightly red as he tucks some of his hair behind his ears. When April said, "just Reece", I thought he told her that as a joke but no – that's what he goes by and that's the only name on his book. Like Beyonce or Cher.

'Please tell me you're working on a sequel?' I put my hands together in a prayer which I regret later but hey, you can't help it when the fangirl inside you escapes.

'I cannot confirm or deny that statement…yet,' he says, and I smile at him as April chuckles. I notice Jonas rolling his eyes, I can already tell we won't get along. 'I'll finish it one day even if it kills me.'

Pluto Retaliating is an amazing sci-fi about the inhabitants of Pluto finding out they've lost their planet status and fighting back against the Earth. The book was published over five years ago, and I know fans, including me, have been waiting for the sequel. I know he's gotten a lot of hate online for not having the sequel ready so it's likely a touchy subject, and I think about how stupid I am for also bringing it up. I'm about to apologise and reassure him to take whatever time he needs but it sounds stupid in my head, so I stay silent.

April gestures that she's heading upstairs so I grab my stuff and join the others in the living room, sitting in the opposite armchair to Reece and feeling motivated to write something, anything. I dump all my notebooks on the floor next to me as my Windows laptop comes to life.

'I haven't published anything yet,' Hallie says, eagerly leaning forward and excited to share. I can tell there's been a lot of silence before I showed up. 'I had to take a few days off work to come. Life of a writer in all, got me two jobs to support it. But I write non-fiction.' This grabs Jonas' attention and it's the first time I've seen him not typing.

'What kind?' he says, his tone sounding more demanding rather than intriguing. I half expected them all to be Scottish but only myself and April are. Hallie has a Welsh accent and the other two sound more like they're from the south, London maybe. Jonas has a hint of something else in his tone and if I had to guess it would be Spanish judging by his name.

'A little bit of everything but right now history-'

'Not about this area?' His tone now sounds angrier, and I see Reece sink in his chair, notepad covering his face.

'Yes?' Hallie says like she's questioning her own work now.

'That's what I'm doing and I'm a bestseller so good luck with that.' Jonas snaps his laptop shut as if Hallie has been looking over his shoulder to cheat from him. 'You'll choke, for sure.'

He says he's a bestseller, not that I've ever heard of him (not that I could possibly know every author on the planet). I'm tempted to ask questions about his work, but I feel it will just add more fuel to the fire or inflate his ego. I'm not sure what would be worse.

'I'm pretty sure someone has already written about the history of this area,' I say, trying to diffuse the situation but I get an annoyed look from Jonas and a worried one from Hallie. 'Doesn't mean you both can't also write about it in your own words. Maybe you can compare notes.' I regret that last sentence, but it's already been said, and I can't take it back.

'Ugh,' Jonas groans in frustration, not looking at any one of us in particular.

April comes back down the stairs with a grin on her face, obviously excited to sit down with other writers and discuss all things writing-related. I can see she soon senses the tension in the room, with Jonas still looking at me with annoyance and Hallie wishing she was sitting anywhere but next to him. Reece is just pretending he's not there by looking at the ceiling.

'Now that you're here,' April says, looking at me. 'I can make some food. I bought a bunch of snacks so we can have a nibble lunch or-'

'Stop right there, we don't need any more options,' Reece says, his neck snapping back to look at April. 'Nibble lunches are superior, now let's get cracking. What do you need help with, and do you need an official tester, just in case?' He's half out of his seat before April waves him down, like a zookeeper controlling her hungry animals.

'No, you carry on working. I already got a head start on my current WIP before you all came.' I see Hallie mouth "WIP?" so Reece tells her it means "work in progress".

'Another edition to the *Ever a Never After* series?' I say, trying to choose which Word document to open as there are about seven of them with different random notes on them. One of them just says "vampires" – whatever that great idea was supposed to be. Certainly, it cannot top the masterpiece of *Twilight,* and no, I am not being sarcastic. Fight me.

'The next one for that is already on its final draft, the editors are just running through it again.' She starts to pull out every dish she can find and fill them with crisps, pretzels, and other salty snacks then she starts making a cheese board of some kind. 'No, this is a new one.'

'Oh?' April has never published anything that doesn't belong to the *Ever a Never After* series and I wonder if it's now a touchy subject. I didn't think about whether she modelled the characters after her relationship – even though she started before they got married but she could have once they were together. 'Since the characters are getting on in age, is the series retiring?' I can't help but ask yet I wonder if I'm being insensitive. If I am, she doesn't show it.

'They are retiring soon – not with book sixteen but maybe eighteen or nineteen. They've lived a good, long life but I would like to look into other stories.'

'If you need a beta reader…' Although I said that genre isn't my thing, she does write good, queer relationships and maybe her new works won't be contemporary. You can learn a lot from reading a little bit of everything, even if it isn't always your cup of tea. Writers' tip number 13.

'You are welcome to read it; I have a printed draft with me which you can have later.' The rest of them have been busy typing (or writing) away while I've been pressing April for news on her work. I decide to close all the other documents and start afresh but end up watching the cursor just sit there on the page. *Does it not blink anymore?* I think and decide to try Googling why it doesn't anymore but remember there's no Wi-Fi. I could hotspot my laptop (like I planned to when sending Spence my crap) but April's right, having my phone not in my pocket does help as laziness takes over and I stop thinking about how important it is to know such information.

'It's not much but, come dig in,' April says. Reece is already by the kitchen island before she's finished her sentence. "It's not much", she says when the entire island is full of food.

After we eat, most of us are in the kitchen discussing our books (or in my case, loose ideas) except for (you've guessed it) Jonas, who grabbed a plate with a quick "thanks" and kept working. April explains some ideas for the ending of her series. When she mentioned killing off one of the characters early, Hallie made her promise not to. I talk about whether a mud monster and a werewolf could have a relationship together. Hallie and April say no but Reece says definitely yes. We silently decide between us not to press Reece on his book, but he manages to reveal the idea is there, but the words are not.

We settle back down again in the living room – ready to work with April cleaning the kitchen. We did offer to help but she declined, I think she's determined to be a good hostess.

I grab one of my notepads and I immediately regret labelling them when Jonas says, '*Writing prompts?*' And he's not asking because he's curious, in fact, he's not asking at all. He said it in a judgemental way.

'Some of us write fiction, where ideas aren't as readily available as non-fiction is,' I say and, if you are reading this as a non-fiction writer, I do not believe that. I just want to get on his nerves. I can tell I've hit the mark as I see a little vein throbbing in his forehead.

Without a word, Jonas gets up (taking his laptop with him) and goes outside. Hallie looks at April, clearly uncomfortable but April just mirrors back the same expression. I can hear Reece stifling a laugh behind his notepad.

'He's certainly an interesting character,' Reece says, finally coming out from hiding. 'I should make him one in my book, but I feel like he would sue me for doing that.'

'Would he be alien or human?' I say, interested in talking anything and everything about *Pluto Retaliating*. April takes Jonas' seat and smiles at Hallie, patting her on the knee like they're mother and child.

'That's human behaviour right there, no aliens like that.'

'*Pluto Retaliating 2: Jonas Strikes back.*' I can only imagine the terrifying book cover for that story.

'Don't do my favourite film series dirty like that.' This is a surprise as, although there is nothing wrong with *Star Wars*, I expected Reece to go for the more horrific side of sci-fi, films like *A Quiet Place,* based on his book.

I'm about to say something else until we hear something coming from upstairs. At first, I just think one of my bags has fallen over with a huge thump, but it continues. It's clearly someone stomping around upstairs, whether it's because they are purposefully doing so or it's just that type of flooring.

'I didn't know you had invited someone else,' I say to April, and I look around to see them all looking up too. When I see April's face, there's confusion at first and soon a slight panic.

'I didn't.' Her voice is a little wobbly and I want to reassure her that there must be some explanation.

'Owner then?'

'It was self-check-in,' April says walking over to the stairs and peering up. 'I said I could meet the owner anytime they wanted but they insisted on leaving the keys under the mat for me.'

'You haven't met the owner?' Hallie says and the stomping becomes quieter – yet we can still distinctively hear footsteps. Then we can hear other noises, shuffling and a scuffle like they're searching.

'I've gone to many places without meeting the owner, self-check-in isn't unheard of.' April says the sentence so quickly she's spitting at the end of it. I don't think Hallie meant to say it judgementally, but it did come across that way.

'Is the owner squatting in their own home?' Reece says, laughing at his own joke. He stops when no one else joins in with him. 'Maybe a cleaner or groundskeeper?'

I think about joining in with him to ease April's mind, but I know now to be more realistic with what's going on. 'Who's been up there this entire time without making a sound until now?'

'And he didn't tell me about anyone else, he said we would have the place to ourselves,' April says, her voice trembling even more now. I see her about to make her way up but pausing when the noise stops. The silence is somehow more terrifying than the noise could ever be. We wait for any sign of life again but there's nothing. 'Hello?' April calls up.

'Shush,' Reece says. 'You ever seen a horror?'

'Please don't,' Hallie says, and I notice her hand shaking a little.

'I think we're safe in this circumstance as we're not the ones upstairs. If we're going by horror stereotypes,' I say.

'And please stop joking.' I didn't mean it as a joke, I was only speaking in facts, but I stop anyway.

'Come on,' Reece says. 'There's four of us and one of whoever is up there.'

'Five of us,' Hallie says, her attention turned from the noise back to Reece.

'What?'

'There are five of us.' There's a beat of silence as confusion grows over Reece's face. April isn't paying attention to the three of us as I hear the bottom step creak from her rocking her foot on it. I can see her mind racing with so many thoughts on what to do but she can't make up her mind.

'Yeah, that's what I said - five.'

'Is he still sulking outside?' I say and Reece turns around, sitting up in his chair to peer out the window. 'Did he go off on a walk?' April snaps out of her thoughts and moves to the window and looks out too.

'You said four of us, why did you say four?' Hallie says and Reece turns back to face her.

'I said five.' His tone sounds like he's defending himself against an accusation. 'Why are you getting so worked up for?' Hallie is already off the sofa mid-sentence, looking at the window with April. She's at least a foot shorter than April (even smaller than me) and because she's on the younger side, they could look like an older and younger sister standing there together.

'He didn't take his coat,' I say as Reece gets up to have a look too. Now he could be the middle sibling of the three, he's likely a similar height to me – maybe a bit taller.

After flopping back down on the armchair after a quick look out the window, Reece says, 'I think we all need to calm down, it probably wasn't anyone upstairs and Jonas was probably too stubborn to come back for his coat before heading off.'

'That's a lot of probably,' I say. I'm the only one who hasn't gotten up because, frankly, I don't care. He's a grown man, he can take care of himself. I'm way more concerned about the noise and how silent it's been for so long.

'And you were pretty sure someone was up there a few minutes ago,' April says, moving to the kitchen window to get another look. Hallie has given up her search and sat down in the same spot. They all seem more worried about not being able to find Jonas than the noise now.

'Fine then, one of us should go upstairs then,' Reece says and it's clear he's not volunteering himself.

'Off you go then,' I say, gesturing to the stairs.

'No-'

'Well, it was your idea,' Hallie says, crossing her arms.

'But-'

'Maybe it was just something falling over-'

'April, don't be silly-'

'Listen-'

A loud thud stops us all from talking.

Chapter 4

There's been a few seconds of silence, no one has dared to speak.

April is the first to break it. 'What is going on?' She asks the question so quietly I can barely hear her. Reece only offers a shrug and Hallie and I don't move, but I can hear her breathing loudly, her heart likely pounding like mine is.

Soon enough we can hear the footsteps again and they start to move out of whatever room they were in. I follow the sound with my gaze and watch as it comes out into the hallway upstairs and pauses for a moment or two.

The noise suddenly moves towards the stairs and unexpectedly Jonas comes down, which is a relief to us all at first, April clutching her chest and Hallie with a big sigh until we realise-

'How did you get up there?' April says as Jonas looks at each one of us in turn, just as confused as we are. He drops his laptop on the kitchen island and looks at the stairs and then at the front door.

'And what were you doing upstairs for so long?' I say but he doesn't look at me and when I get glances of his face as he turns to survey his surroundings, he just looks lost.

Reece asks if he's okay, but he doesn't reply to any of us, instead he walks straight out of the door again, this time slamming it. The three of us stay where we are but we look at April who is watching Jonas. There's a look of confusion which quickly turns into a look of shock. It's not long before we hear someone upstairs again and then Jonas coming down, running this time.

'I can't leave,' is all he says.

'How do you keep doing that?' Reece says, walking over to Jonas. He has a large grin on his face like he's a child at a magician's show.

'I exit through the front door, take a few steps, and then when I blink, I'm suddenly in a room upstairs.'

'Wicked.' Reece claps his hands, amazed at Jonas' trick.

'No, not wicked,' Jonas says, 'why can't I leave?'

Reece stops being excited when he hears the anger but also the slight terror in Jonas' voice. 'Let's see if I can be granted passage.' He says nothing more as he leaves the house. We all scramble to the windows, and I see him one moment, walking down the rocky path but then I blink, and he's gone.

'He's gone!' I say.

'No, he hasn't,' Hallie says but I watch her face and see her blink. 'Wait, now he has.'

'And now for me too.' April says and Jonas stays silent – already knowing he didn't expect anything different.

It takes longer this time for us to hear something upstairs but finally, we hear the scuffle, and then Reece appears on the stairs. 'I would usually think this is cool if this was happening to someone other than me.'

We're silent but I know we're all in the early stages of panic. I don't know what to do with myself, I feel useless and helpless in the situation and to the others too. What does it all mean? How does it work? What does our sight have to do with it? It's like the weeping angels from *Doctor Who* but at least we're not going back in time.

Hallie sits back down on the sofa, and I wonder what is going through her head. I'm surprised she's not trying to leave herself, but I don't make the move to do so either. If Jonas and Reece can't leave, how can I?

I see April, Jonas, and Reece thinking about what to do next. Reece looking out the window for anyone and Jonas shouting out the front door, his feet still inside as he leans out. His voice won't carry to the road, let alone any sort of civilisation. April is just pacing and then looking towards the back of the house.

'Backdoor?' April says as if it's the front door doing it to them. The three of them still try it together, I watch them scramble, almost shoving each other to get out like whoever is first will make a difference but soon they come down the stairs. I watch April's face when coming back down, her first time experiencing the phenomenon. She just looks dazed, almost as if she's unwell.

'Climb out of a window?' Reece suggests.

'What will that accomplish?' Jonas says.

'We'll be tricking the system?' And as ridiculous as it sounds, Jonas still tries it anyway with Reece, one out of the living room window and one out of the kitchen. I'm not terribly surprised to hear them upstairs a while later. 'You were right, that was dumb. Unless...?'

'No.' Jonas sighs loudly. 'We're not trying the upstairs windows.'

Although I almost want to laugh at Reece's idea, I don't and stay silent. April, who has only tried to leave once, has already stopped trying and is leaning against the kitchen island, watching the guys try again and again. She already knows what I know, this isn't going to work. I look to Hallie who is just staring intently into the fireplace, watching the flames crackle and burn.

'Guys,' I say, catching them both before they head out, yet again. I stand in the way of the front door and even Hallie gets up from the sofa, joining us all by the door. They thankfully stop and listen to me. 'Just take a break, please? I've lost count of how many times you've tried.'

'Take a break?' Jonas says, his anger rising to a whole new level. I think he's about to take it all out on me but then he rounds on April. 'What is this place?'

'I don't know,' April says, looking at the ground with what looks like too many thoughts running through her head, 'it was in a newspaper ad and looked good.'

'A newspaper ad?' Thankfully Reece doesn't sound angry at her and is keeping a clearer head than Jonas. 'God, you're old.'

'We're trapped, because of you,' Jonas says, his accusatory finger-pointing close to April's face.

'Maybe we should calm down,' I say, 'and call someone for help.' Hallie says nothing as she makes her way to the box.

'Best idea I've heard all day!' Although there's some sarcasm in that sentence, I feel as though it's masking the panic he is feeling right now.

'Where're our phones?' Hallie says but before April can answer, Hallie shows us an empty box and even tips it upside down in case it's some magic trick. 'Well? Where did you put them?'

'I just bought that phone,' Reece says, crossing his arms across his chest, sulking.

'Who cares if you just bought that phone? I would kill for any old crappy phone if it worked so I could call somebody to get me away from that lunatic.' Hallie points her finger, accusing April of so many things without saying many words. Hallie's anger overpowers whatever Jonas has been throwing at us. April is too stunned to speak, and I can see her shake, her eyes closing on the verge of tears.

'First of,' I say, almost standing in front of April to try and guard her for the others, 'Reece your phone is probably insured, right?' He nods at me and tries to speak but I cut him off. 'You'll get a new one, it's fine. Second, your phones were all in there when April put mine in and she hasn't been anywhere near that box since. Unless one of you wants to say for certain you saw her?' We all immediately look to Hallie who says nothing but does shake her head. 'No? Didn't think so.'

'And thirdly,' Jonas says, reaching into his pocket and producing an iPhone. 'I have a phone and it looks like there is signal.'

'What phone did you put in the box?' Reece says and I remember the brick phone in the box.

'My work phone,' he says, as he unlocks it and starts dialling 999. 'Glad I put that one in your box now.'

I can tell April wants to speak up for herself but stays silent like the rest of us, listening to the dialling tone. Reece starts mumbling about "what sort of writer has a work phone?" but we all shush him at the same time. When the noise cuts off, I steady my breath so I can hear the voice on the other end of the line. I can't hear anything though, yet the dial had such a distinctive noise. I watch as Jonas' face turns to confusion and then anger. Without a word, he hangs up and dials again – but the same thing happens, I hear the dial tone and then silence.

'What's happening?' I say and he passes the phone to me. When I hold it to my ear, that's when I can hear something. Indistinguishable voices, all overlapping each other. Some more like whispers and others like screaming for their life. Hallie grabs the phone to listen and Reece and April question what we're hearing. It's almost hard to describe to them as it sounds insane. Once they've also listened, I ask for the phone back so I can try other numbers. I try Spence, some friends, and even my local pizza place (yes, I know the number off by heart). But it all results in the same and all I want to do is stop listening to the fear coming through the phone. 'Hotspot your laptop?'

Jonas grabs his laptop and sets up the hotspot. He puts it on the kitchen counter for all of us to see. He makes a phone call, and the same thing happens. He tries facetime but when the call connects, it's a dark screen. He calls out to them, but no words come back. He even tries e-mailing someone and gets a reply straight away. There's a glimmer of hope on his face until he opens it fully and the words are unreadable, the words overlapping each other. He tries going onto the internet but it's the same as e-mail.

The rest of us look at each other, thinking about what to do next.

'Nearest house?' Reece suggests while Jonas keeps trying people. 'Maybe we can find a way to contact them?'

'A mile or so away,' April says, not meeting anyone's eye. 'And how do you suggest we contact them? Unless you want to set the house on fire to create a beacon...' It's a bad joke but I almost want to laugh at the situation. 'Burning to death sounds great.'

'Paper aeroplane with the right wind?' Reece and I both glance at his notepad and then at each other but say nothing. I can tell the rest of them aren't in any sort of mood for jokes. Jonas snaps his laptop in frustration.

Hallie hasn't said a thing for a while now, but she's sat back down now in the living room and looking at the floor. I'm not the best at comforting others but I know how horrible a panic attack feels. I lean on the arm of the sofa and rub her back, telling her the breathe. I think she might tell me to leave her alone, but she doesn't.

'Before you were trying different exit routes out of the house,' I say to the others who are still standing around. It wasn't a question, so they don't answer me. 'I don't think it matters which way you exit the house.' The three of them all turn to look at me. Hallie's breathing is more regulated, so I leave her to compose herself and join the others in the entryway. 'You said when you blink, you come back. Right?' I'm aiming the question at Jonas, but the others nod too. 'I have a few ideas if you're all willing to try.'

Chapter 5

Although we're not exactly in immediate danger, it's not like we can go back to sitting in the living room, writing away and pretending that we can leave the house. I already have some thoughts on what we can try and, although they sound ridiculous, trying is better than nothing, right?

I search the house for things, mainly I'm looking for a rope and maybe some other communication device rather than a phone but I'm coming up empty. April confirms that the house doesn't have anything in it besides what's fixated on the ground or walls. I feel them all watching me as I pull open cupboards to double-check, just in case.

'You seem to have some understanding of what's going on,' Jonas says like I am the one keeping him here. For what purpose?

Entertainment, surely.

'I will have some understanding if we try my ideas, you might learn something.' I turn away from him, closing the cupboards and giving up on that but I can feel the annoyance radiating from him. Reece can't help but laugh a little as I check on Hallie. She's still flopped over but her eyes are squeezed shut – the wrinkles around them becoming more prominent. I gesture for the others to gather up, like we're on a football team, near the front door. 'You blink, you return. We could try not blinking but I doubt we would get much further. How about, walking out with your eyes closed?'

'Could we even leave the house if we do that?' Reece says.

I shake my head. 'I don't know until we try.'

'And how do you plan to navigate?' Jonas says, arms crossed. It looks like he has volunteered me for this already without discussion, but I don't argue against it. Apart from Hallie, I'm the only one who hasn't been outside. It makes sense for me to be the test subject.

'I have you all to be my eyes and ears.'

'To a certain point, you do.'

'True but there are public footpaths all over and I saw a couple walking their dog earlier. We just need to flag down one person to call for help.' I pull on my coat and wellies and then survey outside through the door's small window.

Jonas rolls his eyes and looks up to the ceiling, his hands pressed together in prayer. 'Kill me.' He pauses to wait for something to smite him down but doesn't happen. 'Actually, scratch that, I'll kill myself.'

'What do you think is happening to us?' April says to me ignoring Jonas.

'I'm not sure but I've had several thoughts. The one that keeps swimming around in my head is the Taylors,' I say.

'Taylors?' Jonas says with an eyebrow raised.

'I thought you were researching the area.' In the little time I've known him, I've come to realise I enjoy pressing Jonas' buttons. That sounds sort of wrong, I don't mean it like that.

'The important aspects of it,' Jonas says, pushing his glasses up with a puff in his chest.

'One of the locals warned me of potential Taylor ghosts.' I think back to the mirror and wonder if it could be ghosts. I've never heard of a ghost doing that though – not that I claim to be some expert. I would ask somebody to call the *Ghostbusters,* but we don't have a workable phone.

'And you didn't tell us?' Reece says, sarcastically with a smile on his face.

'I would welcome ghosts at this point,' April says, looking more defeated by the second. I put my hand on her shoulder, so she looks at me. I smile at her reassuringly and manage to get a smile back, the first time I've seen one in many hours.

'So, we've angered a ghost?' Reece says and Jonas lets out a long sigh. 'You can roll your eyes all you want, and I'll roll them back to you.' He pauses and looks at us for laughter, but it doesn't come so he continues. 'But how else can you explain what's happening?'

'Witchcraft sounds more plausible,' Jonas says, he mumbles under his breath, but we can all still hear him clearly.

'Is there witchcraft history here?' I say and he only shrugs at me, rather than going into a rant as I predicted. 'Well, you said you were looking at the history of the area, there must be something about Rosemary Hollow if this is happening to us.'

'I could check my notes, I suppose.' When Jonas doesn't move, Reece grabs Jonas' laptop and hands it to him. I expect Jonas to say something but instead, he quietly goes and sits next to Hallie. He even nudges her with her laptop which she reluctantly grabs, and they both sit there, looking through their notes. It'll be a good distraction for her.

'One more thing for this to work. If either of you blink, I'll disappear for you. One of you needs to close your eyes until the other cannot keep an eye on me any longer,' I say, and they agree for Reece to watch first, then April.

I feel the nerves getting to me, realising I am about to experience the feeling for the first time. I nod to my two navigators and close my eyes, opening the door. I step out cautiously, dragging my shoes over the gravel with each step to not trip.

'Well, it works,' Reece says.

'For now, at least,' I say, still taking each step carefully. I would hate to fall in front of them.

'Just go straight until we tell you – don't swerve off left otherwise you'll be going for a swim.' I can hear April hitting him as he exclaims loudly in pain. An over-exaggeration, of course.

I can feel my feet tread over gravel then grass and back and forth again and again. It's clear I'm not sticking to the path but it's so windy, that it'll be almost impossible to do so. I feel a stone in my shoe and wonder how on earth it could even get in there.

'Veer left a bit,' Reece shouts at me.

I stop in my tracks. 'I thought you said not to do that.'

'I said a bit, not a lot.' I do as he says and take a few steps.

'Better?' When I get no response, I stop again. 'Reece?'

'Sorry, I was holding up a thumbs up and April pointed out you can't see me when I explained it to her.'

'Oh Jesus, help me,' I say, continuing. For a while, Reece messes with me – telling me to go left and then right and back again until he goes silent, and April takes over. It's not long before her commands become more distant and less clear.

'I'm having trouble hearing you now,' I shout, and she says something back, but I can't make out what she says. 'I'm going to keep going!' I hear her saying something again and I stop to try and work it out but it's no use. 'I can't hear you.' I don't shout that, because if I can't hear her, she's clearly not going to hear me either. She doesn't stop shouting at me though and soon, I think I can hear Reece joining in too. I should have thought about not being able to hear them after a while, but I didn't think it would be this soon. I can't even tell where I am, I hope I'm near the road (if you can call it that).

I feel like I'm in *Bird Box*.

I'm going to have to pull a Sandra Bullock and rely on my other senses. The only noise I can hear is the wind, whistling through my ears and the rustle it makes through the trees. It must mean I'm at least near the road. I pray someone is walking their dog or on one of those walks for their mental health (which I should really do myself). The crisp air sends a chill through my nose as I breathe and through my scalp too, causing me to wrap my arms around myself.

Then, I can hear something.

Or someone.

'Hello? Hello? We need help,' I say, excitement already coursing through me, but I hear no response. I stop moving to hear whatever it is clearer. It sounds like footsteps, but they sound odd. The best way to explain it is thuds – which aren't quite causing an earthquake but certainly making the ground beneath me shake a little. *Like a landslide.* I push that thought away, I know it to be untrue as the noise is coming from in front of me, not behind. With each step they take, it makes me jump – even though I know it's coming. They're coming closer to me and soon enough, I can feel something circling me. I'm starting to feel like a meal again. Then suddenly, it stops. It stops right in front of me, and I can hear something breathing, the huff of breath lingering over me.

I feel the urge to see what it is – to see what is hunting me. Technically, I can open my eyes, right? I just can't close them again. I can take a peek. I know this means I will end up back inside, but I've been standing here for so long, not being able to move. I can't help but shake with either anticipation or worry or both.

I slowly open them and see nothing. No one. Just a second ago, someone was breathing in front of me. I am absolutely sure of it, I felt it. I scan the area, but I can't see anyone, not even an animal of any kind.

Soon enough, my watery eyes betray me.

Chapter 6

'Something happened,' I say, after coming down the stairs. The sensation of being transported from outside to inside is like a rush. It feels like a weird rollercoaster which you can't quite remember being on. I feel lightheaded for a minute or two but soon back to normal. I wonder if the further away you get, the worst it is. Like the feeling of being in space compared to being in an aeroplane.

Reece and April are by the door, just like I left them. Hallie looks around at me, but Jonas is still hyper-focused on his laptop. I'm about to tell them about what was out there or, at the very least, describe it but April cuts me off.

'Something was out there,' April says and I'm thankful I'm not going insane or at the very least going insane alone.

'You saw it? I could only hear it.'

'Not clearly but we saw a large shadow and worried about a possible landslide. We went to check out the back, but nothing seems amiss,' Reece says. 'When we came back, it was gone.'

'Was it a person?' April says, changing the subject slightly. 'The shape kept changing like it was moving while standing still somehow.'

'I don't know of any person that large. And it was gone when I opened my eyes – how could it disappear that quickly?' I glance out of the window to try and see if something is still there but whatever it was, it's long gone. 'It circled me, like prey.' They both stare at me like I'm trying to make them scared on purpose.

'Maybe it didn't circle you like prey, maybe it was guarding you.' I can tell she's reaching for some over-explanation. Honestly, I'll take it.

'Guarding?' I ask.

'Maybe that's the thing keeping us here. We're prisoners.' It's not an out-of-reach theory at all, it could be a really good explanation.

'But, why us? Why does it want us?' Reece says. 'I know I'm a minor celeb but I'm hardly the Queen.'

'If you're correct,' I say to April and then look at Reece. 'I doubt it matters who we are. What matters is what it wants with us.'

'You were saying you were like prey. What if, it wants to eat us?' I can hear Jonas scoff at Reece's comment.

'Jonas is right,' I say, which makes Reece's jaw drop open and Jonas laugh a little. 'If it wanted to eat us, it would have done so already.'

'That is not why I scoffed, and you know it.' Still not even looking away from his laptop.

'It could be waiting for us to be ripe,' April says, laughing but she soon stops, wrapping her arms around her in a hug. 'Sorry, that was a terrible joke.'

'Well, you're right about one thing,' I say. 'It's waiting for something.' I look at April and Reece and see I've made them worry even more. I decide it's best to not talk about what we did or didn't see and move forward to try and get out before something happens. 'What about the research department?' Walking over to Hallie and Jonas and leaning over the couch to peer at their screens. 'Wait, did you see anything?'

'I got up when they were screaming "landslide", but I couldn't see a thing,' Hallie says. 'Jonas didn't bother moving.'

'If it was a landslide, we would feel it before we see it,' Jonas says, his glasses slipping from his face. 'Basic science.'

'Alright basic science,' I say, and he turns to me with the biggest frown on his face. 'This is where you tell me you found something. Something so useful that lets us leave.' He looks back at his screen and pulls up all his notes so we can all see.

'I've got nothing, as predicted. I told you, I was looking into the history of the area i.e., the landslides not this house-'

'This is where it started though, right?' Reece says. 'There's nothing on the place where it all started?'

'There probably is. If I could actually search on the internet like normal.' He starts aggressively typing, whether he's now plotting our deaths or gone back to work for a distraction – I'm unsure. I decide to take a peek at his screen and see Reece and April doing the same. 'I can feel you all breathing on my neck, could you not?' We don't stop and he grunts out a cry of frustration.

'I also don't have anything,' Hallie says and when I look at her screen, I notice her notes are more extensive and a lot more organised. Colour-coded and formatted into sections so it's way easier to read. I gesture for me to borrow her laptop to look, and she lets me. 'I mean, looking at the flora and fauna of the area isn't going to be useful now is it-'

'What?' Jonas says and I feel a repeat conversation coming on, but Hallie stops him from continuing. I'm only half-listening as I scroll through her notes, her laptop breathing fire onto me as it overheats.

'Look,' she says, turning to him. 'I will change my book idea because frankly, after everything that is happening, I no longer care. I'll give up what I was doing to stop you from going on and on about it and being angry with me. Even though, as Sage already pointed out, lots of people have already written about this place-'

'Please stop rambling in my face. I was only going to say why didn't you say earlier you were writing about the flora and fauna?'

'You didn't exactly give me the chance.'

'Just-' but he stops defending himself for a second and remembers that he cut her off. It doesn't take long for him to compose himself.

'You said the history of this place so I assumed you meant the most interesting history of Three Tree or should I say the only history of this place.'

'You shouldn't assume then.' I can't help but smirk at Hallie back chatting him – April and Reece laugh. 'And there is more interesting history to this place than you think.' She's right, from what I've read of her notes, the place has gone through some interesting phenomena over the years.

They are organised by year, so I finally find the 50s – back where the landslides happened. I figured if I was going to look at any history, I would go back to then. Hallie is unfortunately correct though and I can't see anything of note during that time – no hybrid killing plants or animals going wild. I say nothing though as I shake my head.

'So, it's useless then?' Jonas says, snapping his laptop shut in an exaggerated way. I hope he's broken the damn thing.

'So, you just want to give up then?' I say, handing Hallie her laptop back. He turns around and drapes one of his arms over the back of the sofa.

'Why? Got any more brilliant plans?'

'You think my plans are brilliant? I'm touched.' I knew turning his own sarcasm on him would annoy him and I was correct. He makes a noise that sounds like a growl, probably trying to mimic a tiger but it comes across as a puppy and turns to face away from me again.

I look out the window when I realise how dark the room was getting. I can still see the sun in clear view at the front of the house but it's low in the sky now, almost hidden by the trees. While we still have the light, I want to try one more thing.

'My other brilliant idea involves a phone, and only one of us has one so…' I say, tapping Jonas on the shoulder.

'You're not having my phone.'

'What do you think I'm going to do with it? Take sexy selfies with it and send them to your sister?'

'What do you know of my sister?' This makes him turn back to face me. It was a lucky guess, but he seemed the type to have some sort of sibling rivalry in his life – the overachiever to compensate for the smarter sibling.

'Just let her borrow it,' Reece says, after laughing so much his voice becomes croaky. 'She's hardly going to run off with it.' Jonas reluctantly hands it to me and scoffs but says nothing else. 'What's your thinking?'

'It's not just when whoever goes outside blinks, it's also when whoever is watching you go blinks too, but what if I can still see you? Will you get further if I can?' I turn my back to the window and hold up the phone above my head on front-facing camera mode and move it to the side a little.

'I'll go,' Reece says like he's volunteering to go get snacks not as if he's volunteering as tribute. Hallie and April move towards one of the other windows to see out. As he leaves, I readjust the phone so he's in view. I don't know what effect it will have with myself doing this experiment and the two of them watching him too. I watch him bob along like he's Dorothy from *The Wizard of Oz* following the yellow brick road. I can hear the footsteps grow quieter by the second but can still just about see him.

It's not long before I hear footsteps upstairs. I see the others out of the corner of my eye look up and then hear Jonas sigh with frustration.

'Well, that didn't work,' he says, getting up and peering up the stairs.

'That didn't work then!' Reece shouts from upstairs, almost overlapping Jonas' words. I see Hallie and April move away from the window, their faces disappointed, in the corner of my eye. I don't move, however.

'If that didn't work,' I say, 'how come I can still see Reece outside?' I don't dare to look away from the screen in worry the figure will disappear. He has his back to me and has stopped walking, but I know it's Reece. April moves behind me to get a look.

'I can't see anyone,' she says then looks at me. 'You're blinking though. If you're blinking – how come you can see him still?' She's right, I couldn't take it anymore and had to blink but he's still there for me.

'He's upstairs! She can't see him,' Jonas says. I want to say, "why would I lie?" but I'm trying to concentrate on Reece, or at least the Reece who is outside.

'Uh, new friends?' Reece calls down. 'I can't get out of the room I'm in!' April is already running up the stairs and pulling on whatever door to the room he's in. 'Why did you lock the door? Is this some sort of prank Jonas? It's really not a great one, I'll have to teach you better.' Jonas also runs upstairs and eventually, Hallie does too – all of them shouting at each other and trying to kick down the door. Their voices started to overlap so much it was hard to figure out who was saying what.

'Are you pulling on the door or pushing it-'

'I'm not that much of an idiot! What do you take me-'

'Ouch, my hand!'

'Your hand was in the bloody way! For God-'

'You're the one who is in the bloody way!'

It's hard to distinguish who is saying what, until I clearly hear Reece say, 'wait! Don't break the door down, we'll lose money!'

'I think that's the least of our worries, you absolute imbecile!' Jonas shouts, banging on the door again. 'Are you that much of an idiot?!'

I haven't moved while listening to them all. I start to zone out of the screaming and just focus on what I'm seeing.

The Reece outside is still standing in the exact same spot, with no movement of any kind. I continue to blink, wondering how many I can do before he disappears. I don't know how I'm going to get the others to believe me, but I know that's the least of our concerns right now with Reece stuck upstairs.

'I'll go out the window!' Reece's voice carries through them all but they all shout "no!" in unison.

'Enough of this,' Jonas says, and I hear feet stumbling around. 'Reece, get away from the door.' I hear him take a running start and slam into the door. Now he's crying in pain, and I think he's dropped to the floor. 'Dammit, my shoulder!'

'You're not *James Bond,* you know,' April says as I hear more shuffling around. Probably April making sure he's okay. Reece and Hallie have gone back to banging on the door.

Even with Jonas injured (which is hilarious but also a little worrying seeing as we can't call him an ambulance if he's done real damage), I don't take my eyes away. I decide to get evidence of what I'm seeing, to show Jonas that I am clearly not lying. As carefully as I can, as my hands start to shake, I take a photo of him and can see clearly in the small, preview window that he is in it.

This makes the Reece outside jerk awake.

His shoulders twitch up and his head rolls to one side – and I get the sense of déjà vu. I know I should look away; I tell that to myself, but I can't stop. My hand makes the phone shake even more as he slowly turns to look at me with not Reece's friendly smile but instead, the smile of someone hungry.

I drop the phone in a panic and quickly whip around but of course, Reece isn't there. I hear a loud fumble coming from upstairs, it sounds like Reece has managed to push open the door and has fallen on someone, likely Hallie.

'Would you be so kind as to get your hands off my chest?' she says and I hear him scramble to his feet, apologising profusely.

I pick Jonas' phone up and realise I have cracked the screen. Not badly, but enough to make him wildly angry.

They all come down the stairs, Jonas holding his shoulder. 'A big lot of help you were,' he says to me.

'I wasn't lying, he was still outside,' I say, going to the photos to prove it to him. I find it and hold up the phone to them all. 'See? A photo of the back of Reece, taken while Reece was upstairs.'

'Have you smashed my phone?' Jonas says and I roll my eyes. That is what he focuses on?

'That's hardly important right now and I'll buy you a new one. A better one. With a neon pink case to protect your phone better.'

He's about to say something but April cuts him off. 'It's not a photo, it's a video.'

'What?' I turn the phone back to see and she's right, it appears as a video as Reece is moving in it. I almost think it's a live photo but I'm not touching the screen. I watch the same events re-occur, the figure turning to look at me. 'It was a photo; I took a photo.' They all huddle around me to look and we watch to finally see his face.

It's that grin again, the unsettling grin that covers most of his face. The small eyes with wide pupils popping out from his face – blood trickling down from them and then his mouth and ears too.

'Oh my God,' Jonas says, quickly moving away from his phone like that will protect him.

'Why is my face like that?' Reece says, doing the opposite and leaning in to get a closer look. April's expression is hard to read but she doesn't take her eyes off the screen.

'It's not you,' I say.

'Please turn it off,' Hallie says and doesn't give me a chance to do anything. She quickly locks the phone and lets out a sigh of relief. I hand the phone to Jonas with a small look of apology, and I think he's about to go off on one about the crack but instead, he looks concerned.

'I thought you locked the phone?' he says and Hallie nods, confused by what he's saying. 'So why is the video still playing?' He turns the phone towards us and Reece, on the phone, has gotten a lot closer to the screen. Hallie locks the phone again, but the screen soon lights up and continues to play the video.

'I swear, I really do,' I say, holding my own hand to stop it from shaking. 'I took a photo, not a video.' April looks out the window but he's not there, he's in the phone now. Reece grabs the phone and I watch them exit out of photos, remove the app, and turn the phone off.

'Take that other Reece,' he says, tossing the phone back to Jonas who doesn't catch it and the phone suffers from another crack as it thuds on the floor. 'Whoops, sorry dude.'

'You will be,' Jonas says through gritted teeth as we all lean over the phone on the ground. It landed face up and it's likely it doesn't work now yet we still watch it, just in case. Jonas is the first to turn away. 'It's gone.' Still, we all move away from the phone, leaving it on the floor in the entryway and moving to the kitchen.

'There's so much I don't understand,' April says, rubbing her forehead like all the thoughts are giving her a headache. She starts to pace as she lays out her questions. 'Like, what was that? How could a picture become a video? And how could you blink? It didn't disappear like it should have done.'

I ponder all her queries and I don't have answers to the first two but I'm sure on the last one. 'Because it wasn't Reece.' They all look at me and I decide now is the time to tell them, at least I know they'll believe me. 'I need to tell you all something,' I say, and their expressions quickly change as if I'm about to confess to what's happening. 'No, just let me speak before you all get your pitchforks.' I start recounting the story of myself in the mirror when I got here. Explaining it was exactly like Reece, the same freaky expression and what the loud noise was.

They are all quiet to begin with and then Hallie says, 'this is a lot to take in – I don't understand any of it.'

'We have... doppelgangers?' April says, theorising it all.

'I don't think so, I think it's the same being – whatever it is,' I say. 'A copycat of some kind? It copied me and then Reece. Or maybe even a shapeshifter.' I dread to think it's *Pennywise*, I'm not as smart as those loser kids to defeat it.

'Maybe I'm not Reece.' He decides to do jazz hands like it's some magic trick and we all stop to look at him, his face quickly dropping from a cheeky smile to a worried line drawn across his face. 'That was a joke and a bad one. I am Reece.'

'Oh yeah?' April says, lighting up to rise to this challenge. 'Prove it.'

'What do you want me to do, strip down?' He holds his arms out like he's inviting us to take off his clothes for him. When we don't answer him, he starts unbuckling his shorts, and we all yell at him to stop. Jonas is covering his eyes anyway, just in case.

'What would stripping down prove?' she says while Reece zips himself back up.

'That I'm me!' Reece says like it's obvious and we're all missing the point. He sighs in frustration when April raises an eyebrow at him. 'That thing copied my face and my clothes, but I doubt it could copy what's underneath. God, have none of you read or watched a sci-fi.'

'Oh,' I say, understanding what he's getting at. 'It's not an alien though.' I say it like I'm so sure but really, there is a chance it could be. The landslides could be a cover-up for an invasion of some kind. I reach for Jonas' hands and pull them away from his face. 'Scared of what you might see?'

'Any other person I wouldn't care. I just don't want to see any of, well, that,' Jonas says, gesturing to Reece's whole body.

Reece lets out an exaggerated gasp of shock. 'I have a very gorgeous body; I'll have you know.' Jonas raises an eyebrow at him. 'I'll prove it!' Reece goes to unzip his shorts again.

'No!' We all shout in unison at him, and he, thankfully, stops again.

'We'll take your word for it,' April says, looking up at the ceiling but it's too late, we've already all seen his blue boxers. When she hears the zipper go, April looks down again and shakes her head at him.

'Wait for a second,' I stop and look at Jonas. 'Did you say any other person?' I grin at him and wink. He looks at me, with an even more horrifying reaction than everything else that's happened.

'Okay, now I really want to leave.' He's starting to look a little unwell.

'I take it we're not swapping numbers after this then?' Reece says, not being able to help himself by joining in.

'With what phone?' Jonas says and I watch Reece pat down his shorts, looking for his phone, the look of panic on his face and then he remembers it's missing.

'I'll be getting a new one and put you on speed dial.' I didn't think speed dial was still a thing, but Reece sounds so sure of himself.

'Yeah, no. There's no way I'm giving you my number.'

'Who said anything about giving?' Reece winks and Jonas fake retches at him.

'I don't know how you can all stand around and chat about leaving like we're on a holiday together,' Hallie says. She has her back turned away from us, looking into the living room. Hallie has been quiet for some time, and I didn't realise that until she spoke up.

'Just trying to lighten the mood, Hal,' Reece says.

'Don't do that.' She turns to look at us, silent tears falling down both cheeks. It has all gotten to be too much for her.

'What?'

'Give me a nickname like we're friends – because we're not.' Hallie wipes away the tears as April goes upstairs. 'We could have been friends if we weren't in this mess.' April comes back down with tissues from the bathroom and hands them to Hallie.

'Fine then, I won't give you my number then,' Reece says and I'm about to hit him for trying to make more jokes, but it makes Hallie laugh.

'Any more bright ideas?' Jonas says to me quietly as we watch Reece hug Hallie. I think Jonas is being sarcastic at first, but he's got a serious look on his face. I've put myself in this leadership position without even realising – they're all looking at me for more answers. I don't have them. I don't know how to leave this house.

I only have one other option.

'You've rented the house for two days, correct?' I say and April nods. 'I don't know about all of you, but I've told people I'm here so I'm pretty sure if they don't hear from me, they'll send out a rescue party. At least I hope one of my friends will.' I know Spence will for definite, mostly because I haven't sent them anything.

'Me too,' Hallie says and some of the others echo that.

'How much food do we have?'

'Enough for a few days longer, maybe for four days total? Six or more at a push if we ration,' April says. The way she says "ration" makes me feel we're in an apocalypse. Maybe we are and just don't know it yet. Speaking of food, we haven't had dinner, but I can't bring myself to eat anything right now.

'We can survive with just water for a pretty long time if the worst happens,' Reece says. 'Good thing the kitchen is in working order and we don't have to do a *Bear Grylls* lifestyle of toilet water or worse.'

'Worse?' Hallie says. She's clearly never seen the show.

'You don't want to know,' April says, shaking her head at Reece to stop him from talking.

'We can keep trying to leave if you want but it's night and I'm exhausted right now. We can re-group in the morning and try again.'

'Although I want to keep trying, I know you are correct,' Jonas says, and I'm shocked to see him actually agreeing with me.

'I need a snack,' Reece says as he waves down April who was about to sort something out for him. The rest of them are going through the cupboards and I watch Hallie pull a couple of things to eat but then quickly put most of it back. April re-opens the cupboard and hands Hallie back what she had.

'Eat it, we'll be okay,' April says. 'Sage? Snack?'

'Not for me thanks. But I do need some reading material that isn't my own, got that new book close by perchance?' She points to her laptop bag – which I haven't seen her touch once yet. I search through and find the bound-up manuscript – so professionally done, it could be a book like this. I almost ignore the front page, flicking to see whether she's switched up genre but something on the front page catches my eye and I have to re-read it over and over for it to sink in, for the clogs to tick and for me to say, 'April?'

'Yeah?'

'I didn't know your maiden name was Taylor.'

Chapter 7

I know by saying those words, voices will escalate again – filled with anger. And this time, I will be joining them. Except no words come out at first, I just listen to them, shouting at her, wanting answers, and accusing her of anything and everything. She's a Taylor and she's somehow connected to this house – related to someone who lived here. They're not really giving her a chance to answer as they overlap their screaming, backing her into a corner. I have so many thoughts reeling through my mind, wondering what to ask her first, what to demand first from her. But instead, I find myself wanting the noise to end.

'Stop, just STOP!' They mostly look at me with shock, having not heard me sound this way yet. I walk over and gesture for them to back off from her a bit. 'I'm angry too but just screaming in her face isn't going to solve anything.' I say this to the three of them and turn to April. 'You owe us answers.'

'I know,' April says. 'But I don't have as many as you think.'

I get everyone to sit down in the living room, thankful none of them are arguing with me. I was worried about what could have happened to April if I let them tear into her. Would it have escalated to violence? They couldn't kick her out, if anything they would like to keep her in so they can leave.

'I'll start with the most obvious one, what kind of sick game are you playing?' Jonas says to April, leaning forward in his seat and trying to get her to look him in the eye. She doesn't meet it though.

'I don't know if you'll believe me, but I did not know this would happen, I swear it.'

'Bullshit,' Reece says, so harshly there's some spit flying out of his mouth as he says it. Out of the three of them, he's one of the ones who's kept a clearer head.

'You knew something though,' I say and it's not a question.

'I knew something wasn't right about the house, but I didn't know what.'

I lean forward. 'What did you know?'

She sighs. 'That sometime after my grandfather, Victor, left, the rest of the family never left the house again. There were four other people left in the house, my grandad's brothers Silas and Arlo, and Arlo's wife and daughter. They didn't even leave to get food – the crops they were growing in the field were left untouched. I have no clue what happened to them during the time he left and the landslides.'

'Your family didn't tell you?' I say.

'They didn't know either, the reason he left was because they fought. He regretted it happening and not being able to reconcile before they all passed. Now it's just me.'

'And the new owner? You obviously know them?' Hallie says.

'I don't,' she says and Hallie scoffs. 'It's true. The land was bought a few years after the landslides, they mentioned about trying to re-build for several years but weren't allowed until deemed safe. The newest owner isn't a Taylor or related to me in any way – they can't be, it's just me left.'

'You said you saw it in a newspaper?' I say and I hear her inhale through her nose and let out a big exhale before replying to me.

'That was a lie and not a good one, but I worried you would look the place up if I said I found it online with your phones. Looks like I didn't need to worry about that.'

'Then tell us the truth,' Reece says, clenching his fists and getting more agitated by the second.

'I didn't even know anything had been re-built here, not until I received an e-mail. I didn't even realise what they were going on about at first until they mentioned Three Tree. It wasn't called Rosemary Hollow back in the day; Rosemary was the name of my grandfather's niece. The owner contacted me, knew who I was – a big fan apparently - and explained he had rebuilt the place. They said if I ever wanted to rent the place for writing, I could bring along whoever I wanted, and they would give me a "family" discount.'

'You were targeted,' I say, and April final lifts her head to look at someone, at me. 'It's not weird to you that they e-mailed you, a Taylor, about coming here? The last Taylor? They must know about this place. You being a Taylor must be important somehow but why?'

'Why did you not question any of this? A strange e-mail pops into your inbox and you think it's legit?' Jonas says.

'It *was* legit, I didn't get scammed or anything in the usual sense,' April argues.

'And we were the lucky ones to get involved with this too.'

'If you were smart Jonas,' I say, not caring what I might start, 'you would realise April is stuck here too. If for some insane reason she wanted to trap us here, I doubt she would trap herself in here too. I also doubt that if you knew the previous owners couldn't leave you may think it suspicious, but you would come to the conclusion that the locals had come to: they were shut-ins. Not they couldn't leave because of some unknown weird reason. Maybe witchcraft seeing as you didn't bother to research the place properly.'

'For the last time, I wasn't researching this stupid house, I was researching the area!'

'Settle down, children,' Reece says and lowers his voice. 'I don't mean you Sage, but children sounded better than child.' Jonas still hears him but doesn't bother to talk back to Reece.

'I haven't said it yet so I will now,' April says, looking at us all in turn. 'I am sorry. I am so sorry that I invited you all here – I promise I did not know something like this would happen. I just thought I would be getting the chance to see where my grandfather used to live.'

'How could you know?' Reece says calmly. I'm glad someone else has stopped shouting.

'Will we ever be able to leave though?' Hallie says, not looking April's way but at least she's not screaming at her anymore.

'Someone did,' I say, thinking back to the word re-built repeatedly in my head.

'What does that mean?' Jonas says.

'The new owner may have never stepped foot in the house, but someone did. I mean, how do you build a house that you can't escape?'

'Maybe there is a way to escape then?' Hallie says, reaching, and I think I should have kept my big mouth shut. Getting people's hopes up with potentially false information is not a good idea, particularly when things are already heated.

'Was something amiss in the house when you came in?' I say to April, who I can see is racking her brain.

'No, not really. I mean the fireplace was lit but I thought the owner did that to make it warm for our arrival.' *The fireplace?* I get up and watch it, realising it's been going all day and we haven't added to it all this time. I go and grab the plastic box that had our phones in it and fill it with water.

'What on earth are you doing?' Jonas says but I don't answer him. Once it's filled, I carefully walk over and tip it into the fireplace. 'And the purpose of that? To freeze us to death?' I step back and wait – thinking myself to be ridiculous if nothing happens. But, as predicted, the fire lights back up and is stronger than ever.

'How did you know it would do that?' Hallie exclaims.

'It's what you said to me April, "they managed to save the fireplace". How does a fireplace not get destroyed in a landslide?'

April shakes her head. 'I don't know, I just thought it meant they restored whatever was left over.'

'What does this mean? And how is this connected to being able to leave?' Reece says.

'Would it be insane to say the fireplace has some control over the house? The fireplace wouldn't have been lit when the builders were working,' I say.

'So, if it's not lit – we could leave?' Jonas says. He grabs the box from me and refills it. I know, and I'm pretty sure everyone else does too, the same outcome will happen.

'But once it's lit, I don't think we can unlight it,' I say but Jonas still tips the water into it after spilling it everywhere along the way. We watch it re-light, and I almost think the fire has grown. 'The landslide must have disrupted it; it's been unlit all this time and then someone rebuilt it and re-lit the fire.'

'Why did the owner specifically tell you about the fireplace?' Hallie says and we look at her. 'Think about it, the one thing that could help us get out of here. Why trap us and then try to help us?'

'None of this makes sense – setting aside the supernatural stuff I mean which already doesn't make sense. Why does a house want to trap us?' Reece says, frowning.

'They never should have re-built this place,' April says.

'But someone did. Someone made that decision,' I say. 'But your grandfather could leave, April?' She nods so I go on. 'Which means, something happened after he left. What could have changed?'

'There's always been a fireplace though, my grandfather told me stories of wintertime and them sitting around it. He would try to scare his brothers with spooky tales.'

'How do you go from a normal house to this?' Reece says.

'Witchcraft?' Jonas says, laughing at the inside joke. 'Maybe little Rosemary was a witch.' *Rosemary*, I think. Her name swims around my thoughts, the fact the house was named after her once she died. And it's not just a name, it's an herb.

'Hallie, your notes,' I say, and she hands me her laptop again.

'But you already looked?' she says, getting up to look over my shoulder.

'I did,' I say, opening her notes back up. 'I was looking at seventy years ago though. April, do you know when your grandfather left?'

'Not the exact date but only a few years prior so sometime in the late 40s?' They all gather around me now, as a scroll further back – thankfully Hallie has researched before the landslides. I start with 1945 and work my way forward. It takes me a while, but I finally find what I was looking for – which is something odd.

'Here,' I say and point at the screen. 'There was a drought in 1949 for a few weeks and some of the crops died.'

'And why is that important?' Jonas says, a slightly angry tone to his voice like I'm trying to wind him up.

'Because their rosemary died,' Hallie says, sitting next to me and taking the laptop. She's scrolling back further, for what I'm unsure. She pauses a few times and then reaches the end of her timeline. 'They've always had rosemary growing here.' She mumbles under her breath, and I think only I could hear her.

'Rosemary as in the plant I assume, not the girl,' Reece says.

'Both did but, in this instance, I think Hallie means the herb,' I say.

'You still haven't answered my question,' Jonas says, lingering over Hallie so much he's casting a shadow over her. 'Why does it matter if their rosemary died?'

'Depending on who you ask,' Hallie says having finally stopped scrolling. 'Rosemary can do different things, but I think in this case the theory we want to focus on is that rosemary can be used as protection from evil spirits and also witches.' She looks at me. 'Which is why when Jonas said witchcraft, you knew what to look for.' They all look at me.

I sigh. 'I've written about herbs and their properties and researched them extensively. I am not a witch, nor do I believe this is a witch thing.'

'No, but you do believe the evil spirits thing,' Reece says. 'Now it's clear what we need to do, find the ouija board.'

'Oh, Jesus wept,' Jonas says, dragging his hand down his face.

'Jesus is probably weeping.' Reece looks around at us but we're not laughing at his joke.

'Just shut up,' Jonas says, and then looks at me. 'How does this help us?'

'It doesn't – it just explains part of the past,' I say, and he looks at me with confusion. 'I don't know if I believe the evil spirits thing or not for sure but how else can you explain how the house was fine until their rosemary crops died out?'

'And how,' Hallie says, pointing at her screen, 'rosemary herbs never grew here again. Something happened after that drought to this house and the people in it.'

'Yeah, what happened to them is what's happening to us. History is repeating itself,' April says.

'You don't think this means-'

'No,' is all I say, knowing exactly where Hallie is going with that sentence.

'What?' Reece says and Hallie looks at me. I shake my head, but it doesn't stop her from saying something awful.

'You don't think it means there is going to be a landslide, do you?' We all look at each other in turn. I had been thinking about it for a while but did not want to bring it up. 'What do we do in that situation? Sit on the roof?' I don't want to say that wouldn't do us any good.

'Please stop,' April says. 'I can't think about that, I can't think about dying or even worse, you all dying and it being my fault.'

I put my hand on April's shoulder and squeeze. 'We don't know all of the facts. We only have part of the story so we can't jump to that conclusion. Plus, the landslides happened a few years after the drought – we need to account for that and figure out what happened during those years.'

'We need to figure out who the owner is,' Hallie says. 'We should search the house.'

Chapter 8

I don't say it out loud but searching the house could be a lost cause.

The chances of us getting lucky and coming across a clue like we're in *Scooby-Doo* are slimmer than slim. Especially since I've already done a quick sweep of the place.

I wasn't lying before; I was exhausted and now I'm gone beyond that. It's past eleven at night now and I want to say "can't this wait till morning, it's not like we're going anywhere" but I can't bring myself to. I know we're not in immediate danger or at least I hope my instincts are right, so I just want to reset everything by falling asleep and pretending everything is okay for six hours.

'We can scrap the kitchen for searching,' April says, in a small voice. I know she's still beating herself up about everything but if anyone still wants to be mad at her they can do that later. 'I went through all of it when I got here. If you don't believe me, you can-'

'We believe you,' I say and look at the rest of them, challenging them to say otherwise. I don't think they will, and I only believe that Jonas would be the one to search through it again.

'I'll take downstairs with Jonas,' Hallie says, waiting for any objections from him but none come. 'The rest of you, upstairs.'

'Look for secrets,' I say, and they all look at me with confusion. 'What? There could be a hidden room behind that bookcase.' I point to the one in the living room. 'Or one of the bathroom tiles could be pressed to open a secret storage cupboard.'

'In a re-built house?' Jonas says and I remember saying the exact thing to the man in the village.

'What? It won't be the strangest thing to happen today.'

We split up, the exact thing you're not supposed to do.

I know Reece wants to point that out, I can see it on his face, but he stays quiet. At least we're in groups and not completely alone. It's not like we're in the woods. When the three of us go upstairs, we split up into different rooms, April has the bathrooms and me and Reece the bedrooms.

It's like the decorators just copied and pasted each of the bedrooms because they're exactly the same. Pretty sure I'm in Hallie's room with all the books on flora in her room – I have no clue how she managed to drag all this stuff to the house.

I check my room next and nothing.

The next one must be Jonas' room as there's only a black suitcase sitting on the bed and the rest looks untouched.

I re-group with Reece who looks like he's been standing in the hallway for a while. 'Did you check around properly?' I ask him.

'I think so?'

'That's a no.' He honestly looks offended, but I can tell by his face he's as drained as I am.

'I checked in the most important place – under the beds.'

'Now is not the time for…' I trail off and go back to the rooms without another word, Reece on my tail, questioning me. I'm hardly listening as I lie down to look under the beds.

I get up and Reece looks at me like I'm crazy, so I explain he has a point and then talk about *Four in a Bed*.

'Ah,' he says, stroking his chin. 'So Sage, what rating did you give for how clean Rosemary Hollow is then?'

'That's what you focus on?' I say, walking out to meet April coming out of the bathroom. She looks at us confused so I explain the same thing to her.

'I give the bathrooms a nine then,' she says. 'They have an odd smell. I'm unlikely to come again.' She laughs and I'm glad she's seeing the humour from the situation. 'So, nothing then?' Reece shakes his head.

'Well,' I say, opening another bedroom door. 'You can be trusted April, but Reece can't. I'm re-checking the rooms he was assigned.' They follow me in rather than going downstairs. We haven't heard from Hallie and Jonas so assume they are still looking.

'I was joking when I said I didn't look properly.' I realise we're in his room as he starts to clean his stuff away. I have no idea how he's made so much mess already with his clothes everywhere. I watch April lay down to look under the bed. 'I looked there.'

'Why is there a singular shoe under here?' She pulls it out and Reece yanks it from her. We do a proper search of the room and nothing. 'The other room?'

'Your room,' I say to April as we head there.

'I promise I did actually look-'

'What's weird is,' April cuts Reece off, 'the owner did say I should go with this room for myself, claimed to have the best view. So, I did.'

'Wait,' I say and make them pause by the door. 'That's got to mean something.' I don't give them a chance to reply, I instead go in and start moving furniture around straight away.

April joins in as Reece leans in the doorway. 'You really think it's another hint of some kind?' She says, opening the wardrobe.

I move the bed back and look under the mattress. 'I don't think this room has the best view.'

'Ah, note that down on your *Four in a Bed* feedback form,' Reece says, still not helping us. I walk over to him to complain but I step on a floorboard which makes a different sound. I lean back and forth to make the noise louder and crouch down to knock on the floor. 'And she's gone mad.' Reece says to April.

'It's hollow under here,' I say, and try to rip up the floor to get in there. I bend back one of my fingernails trying and cry out in pain. Reece kneels down and also tries but soon gives up.

'Let me,' April says, using her fist to get the wood to budge and soon enough it does. I may have strong legs, but my arms are like crisps.

'Should have just asked you from the start with those guns,' Reece says, pointing to April's biceps. 'I think I have a splinter in my finger now.' We watch April pull the floorboard out and reach into the dark hole. She pulls out a wooden box with a flower design imprinted onto the top of it. She goes to open it, but Reece quickly stops her.

'Wait, wait.' He lays his hand on top of hers. 'Could be a trap of some kind.' We both frown at him at first but then I think about what he's saying.

'It could be true,' I pause, thinking it over more. 'But so far the owner has helped us and it's really annoying we don't know why.' I gesture to April. 'Let me open it.'

'No, Sage,' she says, yanking the box away from Reece. 'I'm not going to let you play hero and get you hurt. Clearly, it should be me.' We're about to argue with her but she quickly stands, her back to us, and opens the box.

April is silent, with no kind of reaction to what she's seeing whatsoever. Her head bowed and unmoving.

'April?' Reece says hesitantly. 'What's in the box?'

I can't help myself. 'What's in the fucking box?' I mumble and Reece laughs until it's been a few moments and April has still not moved. I take a step back and gesture for Reece to do the same. 'April?'

When she turns around, we embrace for it to not be her.

'It's rosemary,' she says, her face normal.

'Jesus, April, don't scare us like that,' Reece says as we move towards her to look inside the box. 'Wait, rosemary?' April pulls out a dead sprig of rosemary and twirls in it her hand, a small part of it falling to the ground. 'Wow, great secret.'

'It meant something to someone,' I say, disappointed like the both of them. I was hoping for a secret key of some kind that lets us out or some kind of portal. That was wishful thinking.

April gets a tissue and wraps the rosemary in it. 'Seems dumb but I'm keeping it, for now at least,' she says, pocketing it. 'Like you said, it was important to someone so maybe it will be important to us.'

'Wait, something else is in there,' I say and reach in, half worried something might reach out but thankfully I pull out the book with my hand still attached to my wrist. It's a brown, leather book with a symbol imprinted on it. No title or anything, even when I flick to the first page. I start to think it's a blank book but after a few pages, there are some scribbles of instructions. 'I can't read it.'

Reece leans over my shoulder to get a closer look. 'You will need fire, a drop of blood from an animal and human, water hemlock, henbane-'

'A summoning ritual.' April and Reece look at me, so I elaborate. 'Someone summoned evil here. Not just any evil here, this isn't evil spirits – she summoned a demon.'

'Of course, you would know all of this,' he says to me. 'You write this kind of stuff all the time.'

I'm shocked. 'Wait, you've read my books?'

'But why?' April says, still reading the book and not listening to us. 'Why would you willingly bring a demon to your home?'

'I think it's clear she didn't mean for this to happen.' I flick through some more pages. 'I think she was trying to do something else. Demons like this could grant you almost anything, for the right price and if you are desperate enough. At least, in fiction, that's the case.'

'Wait, *she* you said?' Reece says with an eyebrow raised.

'Rosemary. I assume this is her room or was her room, I should say. Hiding things in this way isn't adult behaviour. Plus, this is the smallest room, a child's room. Best room, my arse.'

'So, she summoned something, but it backfired somehow, and they couldn't leave the house. Then the landslides got them,' April says, trying to piece more of the story together. 'Wonder what she wanted.'

'You don't contact the dark world for something small.' I stop looking through the book, the rest starts to get unreadable. Like the author got more insane the more they wrote. I'm about to close it when I feel a lump at the back, so I flick to it, and something drops out.

April picks it up and shows us a torn photo. It's almost a slither of paper as it only shows one man. 'Looks like my grandad but it's not, it's one of the brothers. Silas or Arlo.' She flips it over and there's a clump of hair taped to the back. 'Brighter hair, so Silas.'

'This is not good,' I mumble, and they both look at me confused. 'I think Silas died,' I explain. 'Before the landslides and someone wanted to bring him back.'

'You can't be serious,' April exclaims.

'Can you think of another explanation for keeping someone's hair in a demon book?' Reece says and April stays silent. He's got a point.

'What would you do to bring back someone you loved?' I pause and look at her, but I get no answer. 'Your grandfather, Victor, left. Probably no way to contact him. And then Silas leaves too? Probably couldn't deal with the grief of it all.'

'Wait, back up, why is it not good though? If it did work?' Reece says to me.

'Life for a life.'

'Wha-'

Someone screaming from downstairs makes us jump and makes me drop the book.

We all run downstairs and it's Hallie standing in the hallway. Jonas is running from the back of the house, and he huffs when he sees her standing there, no danger in sight.

'Hallie, what's wrong?' I say and she can't get any words out. Instead, she points to the ground where Jonas' phone has been lying there all this time. 'The phone?'

'It moved,' she says in a small voice, backing away from it.

'It's dead,' Jonas says, walking over and picking it up. He waves it in her face which makes her flinch. 'See? So, stop shrieking-' A long claw hand reaches out, a loud groaning noise escaping as it does, and scratches Hallie's face. Jonas drops the phone and kicks it across the room, landing near the kitchen. We rush over to Hallie who now has a large scratch mark across her face which is bleeding a little. Her hands, shaking, reach to her face to feel the mark.

'B-believe me now?' Hallie says, looking at Jonas through her hands. He opens his mouth the say something, but no words come out.

A noise rattling in the kitchen makes us all still.

We turn to see the phone, unmoving to begin with, lying face down. But then it flies around, low to the ground, and lands, again and again, making a deafening thudding noise on the ground every time it does. We jump on every beat, watching it and not knowing what to do.

It finally stops when it lands screen up.

I can only hear my heartbeat as I wait for something to happen. Hallie's breath has quickened and gotten louder, and the others are still, not daring to make a move. The house starts to moan, and the lights darken as the room starts to move, feeling smaller by the second. The deer chandelier starts violently swinging from side to side so much so it's crashing into the ceiling on both sides.

I then watch as the windows go dark, but I can slightly see through the pooling red dripping down them. I can feel every hair on my body stand up as goosebumps take over, my body causing me to viciously shake.

I see Reece leaning over, retching up something. Jonas falls to his knees, throwing his glasses aside, screaming that something is in his eyes as he rubs and scratches them fiercely. April is holding her head, covering her ears whilst leaning against Hallie, who is still but the blood from her face has increased, and I can no longer see her own skin colour anymore.

A noise from the phone jolts me back to attention. I can hear them again. I can hear the noises from before, the crying and screaming.

Slowly, long dark and bony fingers crack and snap as they crawl out of the phone. Like broken bones trying to mend themselves. There's hardly any skin on them as the whole hand emerges, black fingernails scraping the floorboards. Blood starts to pool from their fingers as their nails snap from pressing into the floor too hard.

I watch as the others stop crying in pain, being able to finally notice the hand like I have. The noises the house is making does not stop though, I can feel my head start to pound.

'Taylors, Taylors all around. Taylors, Taylors *dead* in the ground.' The voice sings it like a nursery rhyme, but not soothing as a parent would. Although it sounds happy, a slight laugh when saying *dead*, it's guttural and I want nothing more than to stab my own ears to never hear that again. 'It's been so long and so boring without company for us.' Then it says in a sing-song voice. 'Let's play some sports.' The tone changes again, this time to an infernal one. 'We won't have long.'

We don't move and we don't have to.

The hand drags the phone across the room, leaving a trail of blood as it slowly comes towards us. The scraping sound it's making as it moves rings in my ears, making my head pound harder and sending small vibrations through my veins. I close my eyes as they feel like they're about to pop from my head. My knees buckle and I drop to the ground with the others doing the same, their heads going through the same agony.

A high-pitched and manic giggle escapes the phone as it edges closer to us. I start to see the hand extend out further as its forearm begins to show.

I open my eyes, and everyone else has theirs closed with screwed-up faces. April is crouching right next to me, her gaze leans down and I notice the pencil still tuck behind her ear.

I grab it, waiting for it to come close, and stab through the hand with everything I have.

It yells, the house shaking from its booming voice. Blood pools fast and heavy from the wound, its fingers dancing and tapping around from the pain.

The hand slithers back into the phone and, without giving it another chance, I grab the phone, open a window, and throw it out as far as I can.

Chapter 9

When I turn back, the house is normal again.

There is nothing amiss – no shaking, no pain, and no blood. The others are getting up from the ground and looking around themselves. It seems like a fever dream that we all experienced together.

'Was it…real?' Reece whispers.

'Yes,' Hallie says, tracing a line down the scar on her face. It's no longer bleeding but still a bright, red colour. 'It was. Why didn't it kill me?'

'What?'

She wipes the blood from her lips. 'I mean, that's what it tried to do just now so why not take me there and then?'

'I don't think it's worth pondering, just be thankful it didn't.' Reece holds a hand to his chest and lets out a large sigh of relief. I disagree in my head, as it's an important question. With more force, it looks like it could have killed her. But the whole situation seemed more like a taunt rather than a funeral.

'Where is it now?' April says and I explain what I did. She reaches for the pencil behind her ear anyway but it's obviously no longer there. They all walk over to the window, and we look out but it's so dark we can't see a thing. 'Is it gone?'

'I hope so,' I say, but not feeling too hopeful. I can hear someone rustling around in the kitchen. I turn to see Jonas going through the cupboards. 'What are you doing?'

'Looking for a first aid box,' he says, slamming one closed angrily when he can't find it.

'I have something,' April says, leaving and returning with a soothing cream. She wipes the dried blood off and then applies the cream to the wound which makes Hallie cry. 'Hopefully, it'll be better in the morning.' What she really needs is medical treatment, it looks deep enough to need stitches.

'I'm sorry,' Jonas mumbles. 'I shouldn't have waved it in your face.' I expect Hallie to say "it's fine" but she doesn't say anything. She meets his eye though and he can't hold it for long.

'Did you find anything down here?' I say and Jonas and Hallie shake their heads. 'Because we did.' I explain to them about the book, the hair, and the rosemary. They both just look at me confused by this. I explain further my theories of what this could mean (I say theories to them, but really, I think I'm right).

'So-'

'Oh, here we go,' I say, cutting Jonas off and rolling my eyes at him.

He pretends I didn't say anything and continues. 'So, if it was summoned all that time ago, why is it still around?'

'Actually,' I say, treading carefully as he starts to look mad, 'that's a good point. In myths, deals are made between human and spirit and once the deal is complete, the spirit vanishes.'

'So, the deal was never completed? Rosemary died in the landslides before she could uphold her end of the deal,' Reece says, looking somewhat pleased with himself and with his findings. 'Does this mean if we complete the deal for her, we can leave?' He looks at us to agree with him and I nod my head. 'Maybe that's why you're here,' he says to April. 'It needs a Taylor to complete the deal. Question is, what is the deal?'

'Wait, Sage. You said, "a life for a life"?' April says.

'I did?' I barely remember that now, seems like days ago we were upstairs searching.

'What does that mean?' Hallie says, her eyes scrunched up to deal with the pain.

I sigh. 'It means, if you want to bring someone back to life, you have to sacrifice someone else for them. A life for a life.'

'And since the demon is still around,' Jonas says thinking aloud, 'it was never a done deal. The guy, Silas, was it? Maybe he didn't get bought back but Rosemary still signed on the dotted line.'

'That means,' Hallie says, opening her eyes, 'we need to sacrifice someone to leave?' She holds a hand to her mouth. 'We're not doing that; I don't care if we're stuck in here for days.'

'You're right, we're not doing that, and we don't know that for sure anyway,' I say, but honestly, it's looking to be the case.

'Reece is right, that's why you're here,' Jonas says to April. *Here we go.* I'm about to tell him to shut up but he talks over me. 'The owner has been helping us because he wants to get rid of the demon too. He couldn't just tell you though, who would willingly come here knowing all this? This all leads back to you, it's you.'

April's face turns white. 'What are you saying?'

'Yeah,' I say, grabbing April's arm and pulling her close to me. 'What are you saying?' He just looks at us, his serious face unchanging. 'Go ahead, Jonas. Go get a knife from the kitchen. Try it, I dare you.' I hear April gulp.

He rolls his eyes. 'I'm not going to kill April. The fact you think I'm capable-'

'You're implying it, you snake,' Reece says then hisses at him for effect.

'Oh no, course not. You would want someone else to do it for you,' I say, reaching down to April's hand. 'Let me make this clear for you, I am capable of killing you though, Jonas, so you can shut down that idea right now.'

He steps back and his eyes widen. 'It wasn't an idea; I was just saying-'

'Stop digging a hole, dude, my God,' Reece says, punching Jonas lightly on the arm. 'Truth or not, it's a no from all of us. Plus, the rules of a life for a life means it can be anyone. Want it to be you?'

'Plus, as I said, we don't know the truth. These are *guesses* at best,' I say and April squeezes my hand. 'I don't think we have a way of knowing everything.'

'Ask it?' Reece turns to me and when I look at him confused, he gestures out the window. 'I'll go grab the phone from outside.'

'No!' We all shout at him in unison.

'Though I hate to say it,' I say, looking at them all in turn. 'It might be our best shot.' I look at Hallie who is now shaking and looking dead at the ground. 'I doubt it would tell us anything though. Let's just regroup in the morning.'

'I'm taking Hallie to bed,' April says, letting go of my hand and wrapping an arm around Hallie. I see Reece about to protest but I shoot him a glance and side glance at Hallie, so he backs off.

'It's a good idea,' Jonas says, not looking at any of us. 'We should all go to sleep for now.'

Hallie looks back at Jonas. 'She'll be staying with me all night,' she says, her eyes sharpening when she looks at Jonas. 'So, as Sage said, try it if you dare.'

The look on Jonas' shocked face brings a smile to my own.

I'm in a deep sleep when something shakes me out of it. And I mean, literally shakes me, but when I sit up, no one is there. It was probably a dream, the type that feels so real, but it isn't. My brain is so fried, and I feel so dizzy like I haven't had a drink in days. Without my phone, I have no clue what time it is but it's the dead of night at least, with no sign of any sunlight. Unless the house is playing more tricks on us now. I climb out of bed, open the window, and look out, listening to the whistling wind and feeling the sharp sting of winter on my face. I then hear the crunching of leaves. I expect it to be one of us, trying to leave again in the middle of the night. I lean over the edge of the windowsill and whoever it is, they are too small to be an adult. I think at first my mind or the house is playing tricks on me.

'Hello?' I call out to them, but they do not turn to look at me, instead, they continue to walk around the house. I run to everyone's room, hoping this is no trick, and wake them up – quickly explaining what I saw. Most of them jumping out of bed, looking out their own window before running down the stairs, one of them being annoyed I woke them (can you guess who?). Thankfully, if it isn't a trick, everyone can see the child. They're now walking around the side of the house, past the kitchen windows.

'Help us! Help us please!' Hallie shouts at them and April and Reece join in. When Jonas finally wakes from his slumber, he joins in too – screaming anything to get their attention, waving his hands too as if the sound is a problem. Hallie starts to bang on the window and Reece opens one of them, leaning out and trying to grab the child but they're not within reach.

I just watch the child continue to walk and suddenly come into view through the front windows. But they are not walking towards the front door, they are now walking away from the house – down the hill but not following the footpath. Now they are in clearer view, dressed in a white cloak coat, with the hood up hiding their face and what looks to be like slippers but it's hard to see their feet for certain. I start to notice something as I watch them walk in the tall grass – they are not wading through it; they are just passing through it. The grass is not moving to their body, it is still except for the wind.

The others have stopped shouting, not noticing what I am seeing so I open the door and lean out, my feet still inside and I shout, 'Rosemary!'

I can't see the other's faces but I imagine them to think me insane. But it does what I hope it would do, it makes the child stop. It makes Rosemary stop and turn to face us. Thankfully, her face is normal, or from what I can see of it. Not a sinister look on her.

'Sage…' April's voice drifts off and when I look at her, she's pointing at me. I'm confused at first as to what she's referring to but then I see an arm coming out from me and it doesn't belong to me. I step out of the doorway to see someone standing where I was standing, leaning out the doorway. It must be Rosemary's father, Arlo, and, although he's not making any noise, he looks like he is shouting. I get closer to him and see the worry on his face, a bead of sweat rolling down like he's just run for his life. I watch his mouth and can make out what he's saying – it's "Rosemary", repeatedly.

I go to the window where the others are gathered and look out at her but she's saying nothing back while continuing to stare at her father. I try to think of what I can say to get her to come over here, but I forget that she is gone.

'Taylor ghosts,' Reece says, looking between the two of them. I watch him hug himself like he just felt a shiver on his bones.

'If I die here,' April says, 'will I stay tied to the house then? Like them?'

'I don't think she is a ghost,' I say, and this is when Rosemary turns back and continues to walk away from us. Her father has run out to her this time, but he doesn't reach her.

'You think a little girl and her family from seventy years ago are alive?' Jonas says, not looking at me as he says this, but I hear the silent scoff. We watch the father tumble down the stairs and try again but she's even further away now.

'I didn't say that.' I look around to see her mother at the top of the stairs as the father rushes down one more time. He doesn't leave the house again though as he knows it is useless.

'What is she then?' Hallie says, finally taking her eyes off Rosemary.

'A memory.' The mother has now joined the father by the door, he is still shouting Rosemary's name, but the mother is mute, and her expression is unreadable.

'Memory.' She almost says it like a question, but I don't think she's asking us. She's directing it to herself. We all look at Hallie, her eyes fixated on the ground now.

'You think we're being shown something that happened?' April says.

'At least I'm hoping that's the case,' I say, and Hallie is still mumbling the word "memory" to herself.

'Why?' Reece says, smiling. 'Afraid of ghosts?' Trust him to try and make jokes in any sort of situation.

'No, I'm not. I welcome ghosts but this is odd behaviour. Ghosts don't tend to act this way, it's like they are re-enacting something that happened.'

'Memory!' Hallie shouts at us like it all makes perfect sense. Jonas raises an eyebrow at her, just as confused as the rest of us by her sudden outburst. 'Sorry, I just remembered. In some folklore, rosemary holds memories.'

'Of course! Why didn't I remember that?' I say, annoyed at myself.

'But we only found dead rosemary,' Reece points out.

'It can still hold memory, dead or alive,' Hallie says.

'But I'm guessing that's not the case for protection?' Jonas says, bringing back the memory of the hand coming from the phone. Hallie nods at him. 'Great.'

'So, we unlocked a memory?' Reece says. We all look out the window again and just barely see the glow coming from Rosemary.

'What I want to know is, how has she left the house? And how has she not ended back upstairs like her dad? She's been outside for quite a while now,' Jonas says and they're great questions, but I have no answers.

'And I think your theory was right, Sage,' April says. 'Silas isn't here. I mean, he could have left like my grandfather but why keep his hair? He must have died.'

'One thing we haven't talked about yet – why are they so worried about her leaving?' Hallie says.

'Yeah, she's left the house – isn't that a good thing? She could go call for help,' Reece says.

'Why is she heading to the lake then?' I say and they all follow my gaze to see Rosemary barely in view now. 'Upstairs.'

We all rush up the stairs, leaving her parents still at the door – unable to move, the whole situation out of their control now. We split up, some of us going into one of the front rooms and the others into another. I pull open the window and myself and April lean out of it. I glance over at the others doing the same.

Rosemary is in clear view now; her destination is clearly set for the lake. Her cloak-like coat acts like a beacon.

'What is she doing?' Jonas says, pushing the other two out of the way so he can get a clear view. I can hear Reece mumbling something to him, but Jonas ignores him. They continue to shove each other until Hallie comes into the room April and I are in.

'Going for a swim, clearly,' Reece says as they finally stop fighting.

'When I saw her face, it was blank,' I say. 'I don't think she's in control of what she's doing.' April steps away from the window and I look at her face, her eyes glazing over as she's drifted into thought. 'April?' She looks at me, snapping out of her daydream.

'I know why they were worried,' April says. 'I remember something my grandfather said about her – as they all used to swim in the lake except her. She never learned how to swim.'

'She's going to drown herself?' Hallie says, her voice wobbling and her face scrunching a little like she's about to cry. She holds back the tears though. 'She can't be more than twelve years old.'

'I had wished she didn't die in the landslides but this?' I say, feeling like I had wished drowning upon her. It's hard to remember this all happened seventy years before now.

We're all silent as we watch the bright beacon submerge into the darkness.

Chapter 10

When we get back downstairs, the memories are gone, and the room is still.

I want nothing more than to go back to sleep but I don't think I could if I tried. The nightmares wouldn't allow me. Plus, I don't want to be alone right now. I don't think it would be appropriate to ask any of them to sleep in the same bed as me seeing as I've only just met most of them. Even though it feels like I've been here days with them all not hours.

I could have asked April and the other three if we could all bunk together. I would love to see that dynamic. Thinking about it puts a smile on my face, for at least a moment.

'We have more of the story now,' I say, sitting in the armchair and the others joining me in the living room. 'But not many more answers.'

'It showed us she drowned; she wasn't killed in the landslides but why? Why show us that?' Jonas says, crossing his legs and leaning forward in his seat looking at me. 'You said, "I don't think she's in control of what she's doing." It sounds like you're talking about-'

'Possession.' I finish the sentence for him. Which all leads back to the demon theory but for what purpose?

'You're right,' April says. 'There aren't any more answers, just more questions.'

'Yeah like, what's the point?' Reece says. 'If it is possession, why drown her?'

'I don't think…' I trail off but they all look at me to continue my thought, so I do. 'It's like Hallie said, "why didn't it kill me?" Maybe it can't just kill you, maybe it has to possess you to do so.'

'Then why didn't it possess us there and then? And I'm still confused, why drown her? Just because she couldn't swim? If she was possessed, she wouldn't have been able to save herself anyway.'

'Just raises more questions, doesn't it?' Hallie says, sorrowfully. We all sit there and look at each other in turn.

The clock lets out a loud chime.

'It's two am,' Jonas says, sighing. 'Maybe we should regroup in the morning. Again.'

'Are you kidding me?' I say and he looks confused by my anger. 'We've been downstairs for most of the day and that clock hasn't made a single noise, not even ticking, and now out of the blue, it does. Did you not notice?' The rest of them clearly didn't notice as they look at the clock with confusion.

'Wait, what?' April says, getting up to look at the clock. She puts her ear near it to hear anything, but it makes no other noise.

'I did notice; however, I think a broken clock is the least of our worries,' Jonas says, getting up and going upstairs without another word. April gestures we should do the same, but Hallie doesn't move.

'Reece?' Hallie says carefully and I've not noticed him grab his pencil and pad and start writing.

'You're writing?' I say, scoffing. 'I know you can't help when inspiration strikes but now is hardly the time.' He doesn't look up, doesn't even acknowledge me in any way. 'Reece?' Nothing. He's hyper-focused on his work. I can't even see his eyes as his hair droops down to cover most of his face. 'Reece!' First, the scribbles are quiet, but they soon start to pick up, leading to him writing frantically.

I rush over to him when I see the blood pooling from his hand.

'Reece!' I try to see where the blood is coming from, but I can't make out any sort of cut and even a broken pencil wouldn't make this much damage. And, besides, it's not even broken. The blood soon starts to change colour in places, dark and dried around his wrists and red and fresh all over his fingers. 'Reece, please say something.' He still won't even acknowledge me. I look at his notes but they're unreadable. There's no coherence to it, the words overlap each other, and it looks more like a children's drawing if anything. Blood starts to drip and smear on the pages hiding the manic scrawls.

Once he's finished with a page, he rips it off and lets it fall to the ground.

'What's happening?'

Jonas is standing on the stairs, leaning over the railing at us. I explain what's happening and Jonas just rolls his eyes. 'He's writing, how horrifying,' he says in a mocking tone.

'Oh, shut up,' I say, 'he's not just writing, he doesn't look in control.' I stop and remember it wasn't that long ago that I said those exact words. 'Like Rosemary.' Jonas comes down the stairs and the three of them look at me. 'Oh no.'

'What?' Hallie says her voice wobbling.

'Rosemary was led to a lake and drowned and Reece…' I trail off, not knowing how to end the sentence but I don't need to.

'What does this mean for Reece?' April says and we all look at him.

'Writing is hardly going to kill him,' Jonas says, tapping Reece over and over again with no response.

'Funny, I used to say the exact opposite about it.' April looks ashamed of herself for making such a joke and the real funny thing about it is, that Reece would have laughed at it. He's getting faster with his writing, ripping off more sheets as he goes. The blood has made the pages stickier.

I try to grab one of Reece's hands to stop him from writing, but they're locked around the pencil. I gesture for the others to help but there's no use, not even April with her guns could move him. I watch his hand move across the page and I realise something. 'He's writing with his left hand…'

'And?' Jonas says irately.

'He's right-handed.' I don't think I need to explain that it's not Reece writing, it's something or someone else using him to do it.

'That's it, I've had enough of this.' Jonas leaves the house, and I can't help but roll my eyes at the door as soon enough, I hear him upstairs. 'At least there's a shortcut to upstairs.'

'He's made a joke, I didn't know that was possible,' Hallie says, mumbling under her breath.

I go to the stairs to shout up at him. 'Get the fuck back down here, how can you walk away from what's happening right now?' I get no reply, I guess he doesn't care if it isn't happening to him.

'Oh God.' Hallie quickly moves away from Reece and bends over retching. Thankfully nothing comes out. I go over to see what she's reacting to and can see how badly Reece's hand has deteriorated so quickly.

It's hard to see at first with the blood covering his entire hand but his skin is starting to peel back and show bone. Pieces of his skin start to unravel and fall to the ground. I check his other hand, which is thankfully normal, and wonder how is he not screaming in agony?

April can't take her eyes off of him.

I, carefully, grab Reece's face with two hands and lift his head so I can see his eyes. They're how I expected them to be, like Rosemary's. Lifeless and dull, almost a grey colour. 'Reece?' I tread carefully with calling his name, a little scared of what could happen. Rosemary was no threat, but she was already dead. Reece is, or I at least hope, still alive. I'm about to lower his head but his eyes pop forward, filled with life for only a few seconds. His face screaming in pain at me.

I jump back and scream myself, letting his head drop fast and hard. 'Reece? Reece!' But when I check his eyes again, they are gone. I even wait for a few minutes, but nothing changes. I let go of him gently this time and walk away to see if Hallie is okay.

'I can't look at him again,' she says, gulping and then breathing heavy. 'What is happening to him?'

'I don't know,' April says, coming over and guiding Hallie to the kitchen. 'Let's get you a drink and a snack to calm your stomach.' They sit at the kitchen island together after grabbing a drink and an apple each. April continues to look over at Reece, but Hallie is looking dead straight ahead out of the window. I look at April and I know she's thinking the same thing. Knowing that Reece is in pain and there's nothing we can do is awful. We can't even get help.

'If we could just get the pad and pencil off of him,' I say, trying the pad this time and I know it's no good. I then try to think through ideas of how we can do that. Strength is out the window but maybe a way to break possession? I can't think of what would be in the house that could help us. I shift through the papers to see if he's managed to get a secret message through but there's too much blood to see anything.

The clock lets out another loud chime.

'It's not even on the hour?' April says with an eyebrow raised. 'That thing is really busted.'

Hallie takes a bite of her apple. 'Yeah, what's up with-' She starts to cough mid-sentence. At first, it's small but as it gets louder and more aggressive, April rubs Hallie on the back asking if she's okay. Hallie clutches at her throat, almost clawing at it.

It's not long before the coughs turn into her full-on choking.

April drops her apple and grabs Hallie from behind to give her the Heimlich, but it does nothing to stop the noise coming from Hallie. She starts to really dig into her throat and marks herself all over.

'Why's it not working?' April says, letting Hallie go and not meaning to let her drop to the ground. I run over to help April pull Hallie up, but she's become dead weight.

I'm surprised to see Jonas running down the stairs. 'What's going on?' We don't say anything to him as he watches us struggle with a choking Hallie. He rushes over and tries to help us too but it's like she now weighs ten times what she usually does.

April tries to give her the Heimlich again but it's too late. The coughing has stopped, and she slowly goes limp. Hallie's throat and neck have become blue, her veins turning red, popping through her neck. Her eyes are so bloodshot there's a little bit of blood running from them. She's become so bloated that her face and fingers in particular are much larger than before, fluid dripping out of the seams of flesh.

'Hallie? Hallie!' April cries out, tears streaming down her face.

Hallie's head flops to one side and the little piece of apple falls out.

We're silent. The only noise we can hear is coming from Reece, writing. He's still going, not having stopped once during this entire time. I start to smell something funky, immediately thinking it's Hallie which is crazy. But there's only one other time I've smelt that kind of smell. When I found a dead wild animal in one of my bins.

April is sobbing into Hallie's chest, not being able to stop the tears from coming now. I'm too in shock to react straight away, trying to piece together something that makes sense from any of this.

The smell gets stronger, so I lean down and catch sight of Hallie's face. 'April, I would move away from her now.'

April lifts her head to look at me first in confusion and then looks at Hallie. She screams and drops her, making her thud to the floor, her head rolling to one side to face us.

Hallie's skin is moving, her bloated features deflating into herself rapidly and showing her skull more clearly. The colour sapped from her face as one of her eyes pops oozing down onto the floor. The other eye starts to beat like a heart in her head. There's almost not much skin left and what's there is stretched too thin. She looks like she's been dead for days not minutes.

'How is this possible?' Jonas says, leaning down to look at the apple piece but not daring to touch it. Likely, not daring to get too close to Hallie either.

And soon enough, it hits me.

'You told her she would choke.' I meant to say it in my head, but I say it aloud. April gets up and gets me to look her in the eye. Her face is completely wet and a little red.

'What did you say?' Her voice is now angry rather than sad.

'Jonas. He said Hallie would choke.' We both turn and look at him, and he immediately raises his hands in defence.

'I didn't mean it like that, I *thought* she stole my ide-'

'"I'll write it even if it kills me."' April says. We don't need her to clarify. We all turn to look at Reece who still hasn't stopped writing during this entire time. 'He said it,' she points at Reece, 'and it's coming true. You said it to Hallie,' April points at Jonas, 'and it came true.'

'But-I-I-I didn't-' Never seen Jonas so flustered and worried in my less than a day of knowing him.

'I know you didn't know but I'm just stating what it is. Words have more meaning here than in usual cases.' She pauses, thinking it over. 'Rosemary.' She pauses again for a moment. 'Rosemary or someone else must have said something about her going for a swim.'

'But Reece said that over twelve hours ago now,' I stop, looking at the clock to count the hours. 'No, exactly twelve hours, I came downstairs just before two pm and the clock chimed at two am. Then Reece started to write.'

'And it chimed again not long after,' April says. 'You must have told her to choke not long after Reece said what he said.' I nod. 'Twelve hours...' She trails off as we're just standing there, a body on the ground and someone else possessed and still continuing to write.

There's blood all over his legs now, dripping down to his feet. 'We have to think about what we've said.'

'What good will that do?' Jonas says, crossing his arms.

'I don't think it's going to do us any good,' I say, and they both look at me. I don't elaborate and I don't have to.

'So, that's it? Do we give up? Again?'

'What do you propose we do then?' He says nothing to this, so I continue. 'Sick of you shitting all over my ideas anyway. Cause you're right, they've done fuck all for us.' He's silent, not coming back at me with any kind of counterargument. 'Time for your bright ideas Jonas, come on, let's have them then. We're all *dying* to hear them, clearly.' He looks away from me now, crossing his arms and leaning against the kitchen island. April lets out a small sob, but I can't stop now. 'We're still waiting.' He doesn't move, his eyes going into a blank stare like he's no longer listening. 'Well? Well? Jonas, use that big brain of yours and get us the fuck out of here. Go on then, say something you fu-'

A loud snap stops my rant.

Chapter 11

We all look around to find the source of the snap.

Reece has now run out of paper but that is not stopping him from writing. He's covered in blood now, all over both of his hands, his thighs and the chair and floor too. There's notebook paper covering the ground around him, dried blood all over it. He's now just writing on his leg, digging the pencil into it. I thought it was the pencil that made the snap.

It's not, it's one of the bones in his leg.

He's broken through the skin, created a big opening in the top of his thigh and pushing through the insides. When I get closer, I can see part of the bone poking out of his leg.

'Oh God,' April cries, turning away when she gets a good look. Jonas turns away too, silent but his ashen face says it all.

'I think,' I whisper, worried about what else is listening in, 'he's going to keep going until he actually dies. Whether from blood lost or God knows what else.'

'He's lost so much blood already; how much longer can he go on?' Jonas says, not looking at him again. They've both moved back towards the kitchen, so I join them. April sits at one of the stools and I elect to stand with Jonas, leaning against the counter.

Three of us left, like the final girls. I can hear that statement screaming in the air.

'I'm sorry,' Jonas says, looking down at the counter. I look at April in confusion and when we say nothing to him, he looks up at me. I raise an eyebrow at him. 'I'm sorry for going off at you, giving you a hard time and all that. I-'

'Please stop,' I say, holding a hand up. 'This feels like an unfinished business speech.'

'That's not-'

'I get your anger, I do. But you're not the only one in the situation.' He goes to defend himself, but I stop him. 'Let me finish.' He shuts up. 'And I get everyone reacts differently but getting at me isn't going to help. I just wanted to help, to do something and you jumped at me every time you got a chance.

But you know what?' I put my hand on his shoulder. 'None of that matters now, none of it. So, if you want to hear "apology accepted" fine, apology accepted.' He seems content with that, I even get a small smile out of him. I take my hand off his shoulder. 'You're still a dick regardless though.' He drops the smile and pulls a face at me.

April laughs for a few moments, forgetting everything for just a second but stops and sniffs the air. I watch her gaze go to Hallie and I follow it to see Hallie is in a much worse state. She's decayed, even more, her skin almost gone, and her other eye has disappeared. She's almost just a skeleton now, not much sign left of Hallie in the bones.

Like something has eaten her.

I can see April struggling to look at her, so I go upstairs and come back with a blanket. I cover Hallie up and they both come over to look at the body under the blanket.

'I feel like,' I start, but something catches in my throat, I gulp and continue, 'words should be said. I'm not religious or anything and I don't even know if she was.'

'I don't even know if she had family,' April says and then glances at Reece. 'Or if he did either.'

'Does,' I mutter.

'Did,' Jonas says. 'I don't think it's going to do any good hoping otherwise.' I want to fight for Reece, fight for some kind of hope. But who am I kidding? There is none.

'I don't know much about any of you,' April continues. 'Is it morbid to ask what you would want if-'

'When,' I say. 'It's not exactly looking good is it.'

We all look at each other to say something and I'm stumped. I've avoided funerals my whole life despite it being filled with them. I would say I had deadlines which of course was a lie, and everyone knew it. I made my own deadlines. I can't stand the grief of it, the pain of going through it all again when I've already made peace with it on my own.

I say goodbye on my own terms, and I had already said it to Hallie.

'Rest well, wherever you choose to be,' April sobs, and I hold her, not knowing what else to do. Jonas just stands there, stiff but still staring down at the blanket. April manages to pull back the tears, her face still wet so much so it's left a wet patch on my shirt. 'What should we do now?'

The clock lets out another chime.

'No, no, no, no, *no!*' Jonas shouts, stomping over to the clock and yelling the last "no" as loud as he can. 'What now? What do you want?'

Of course, the clock isn't going to answer him. He even grabs it with both hands and shakes it. I think he's about to break it, whether on purpose or accident but he pushes it back and hits it. He regrets that as he peels his hand away, cradling it.

The fireplace spits out a flame and it lands on the rug in front of it. At first, I think it will fizzle out, but it soon flares up and creates a small fire.

'Jonas!' I shout but he's already there, stamping it out. It works but soon the fireplace spits out another and then another. It has Jonas stomping around like he's in a hoedown.

The fireplace stops when Jonas stamps out the last one. We watch the fire, waiting for more splatters of fire but there is no movement except the usual crackling of flames. Jonas bends down, leaning close to the fire to inspect it.

'I wouldn't do that,' I warn him, and he says nothing in return, just waves me off. He lingers there a little too long like he's looking for the magic behind the trick. It's a plot for disaster playing with death like this. He straightens himself up again and faces us, his cheeks a little warm.

'See? Nothing to worry about-' He cuts himself off by screaming and he quickly drops to the ground and rolls, hitting against the coffee table. Behind him, the fire has grown, and the flames start to evolve into a shape. I lean against the back of the sofa as April pats the fire on Jonas' back. The fire forms into a mouth which opens, bearing its teeth, and a long, flaming tongue with a fork in the middle reaches out. I look at Jonas and April but they're not paying any attention as they fumble off the floor and struggle to the kitchen together. I don't take my eyes off of the fireplace, but I can hear the kitchen tap turn on, likely for Jonas' burns.

I watch as the tongue hisses and then licks its lips. I freeze, waiting for it to grab and consume me in one bite. Its teeth drop into view suddenly, razor-sharp and gnawing at me, cutting through its own tongue.

Then, it vomits.

Fire spewing onto the rug and coffee table, growing quickly. It reaches Reece's feet, but he doesn't react. I go to grab him but the fire flashes at me, pushing me back onto the floor. I crawl backwards until I hit the kitchen island.

'Jesus!' April wails, already filling the bucket with water, but we already know the outcome of this, we've seen it before. Still, she dumps the water onto the fire, and it just grows more. 'Why is this happening?'

I had been thinking about it for a while already and couldn't stop myself from saying it out loud.

'"Burning to death sounds great"' I quote, and I turn to look at April who looks bewildered at first but then her eyebrows drop, and her lip starts to wobble.

'No,' is all she can manage to say.

'She was joking!' Jonas said to us and then looked up and around him at the house. 'God, doesn't this house know sarcasm?' I assume he's posing that question to the demons. The fire reaches the sofa and the opposite armchair, also rising up onto the bookshelves too. We move further into the kitchen together.

'We're going to burn to death?' April whimpers.

'No,' I say. '*We* aren't.' I glance at Jonas and then I look her dead in the eye. A tear slides down her face. 'I'm sorry,' I whisper. I sound like I'm the one with the knife in my hands.

A loud clank followed by a hissing sound comes from the kitchen. We watch as the switch on the wall is flicked and the knobs on the oven turn slowly. We jump when the oven door slams open and crashes onto the floor, coming off its hinges.

There's no logic behind it but we run.

We run, throwing open the door, knowing full well we'll end up back upstairs.

I don't recall closing my eyes.

Chapter 12

There was a bang, maybe.

It felt like an explosion, and it probably was. The air stinks of gas and burning. I'm lying on the grass with my eyes closed, my back crumbled in pain. I remember hearing their voices, calling my name but I couldn't will myself to open my eyes.

I blink several times to re-adjust focus and see that the house has quickly been engulfed in flames. The living room window smashes, glass flying everywhere so I quickly get up and step back. I blink and blink again to see that I have escaped, I have survived.

This is not a victory though.

I look around for April and Jonas, but I already know they are back inside. I run to the door, never predicting I would be wanting back into the house. No matter how much I push, shove, and kick it, it doesn't budge.

I go to where the living room window was and look through to see Reece, still in the same spot, his back to me and his shoulders moving – he's still writing, even now. I want to call out his name, but I don't waste my voice on him, he's already gone, and I know it.

I run to another window, and I see a figure in the kitchen, just standing in the flames. They're burning but not even screaming. I pound on the window a lot, so hard that my wrist and hand starts to hurt, and they turn to face me.

I can barely see her but there April stands, tears streaming down her face.

'April! Get out of there! April!' I feel some hope when she looks at me, but she still doesn't move. She cries harder as I see her legs shake. I grab a rock and smash the kitchen window and climb through, feeling the pieces of glass stab into me. I snatch the blanket off of Hallie and go to cover April, but I blink.

My head hits hard on the ground and my hands touch the grass. 'You have got to be kidding me.' I climb through again, doing my best to not blink but the smoke betrays me, and I close my eyes, tears falling from them. I go to try again but the fire is raging too much in front of the windows and I can't make it through. I can barely see April through it all.

I watch as her skin blisters and peels and burns leaving black, dark holes all over her. Now she starts to scream, calling my name over and over. I pull down the curtains before the flames get them too much and pat down the counter to see April. Her body is charcoal, crumbling apart as she drops to her knees. Her face is stuck in a screaming position, with no movement, just her mouth opening wide, crying in agony. She's still screaming though, the sound echoing through the house and ringing through my ears. It's my name, she's begging me over and over. I look away, not being able to watch her die anymore.

With the horrors of April, I had forgotten someone.

'Jonas? Jonas!' I shout through the living room window but he's not downstairs or at least I don't think he is, it's hard to see. *He could still be alive.*

Upstairs, he's got to be upstairs. Far away from the fire, he can't be burning from the fire.

I back up so I can see through the upstairs windows, but I see nothing so run to the back of the house, hoping to catch some sort of glimpse of him. I hear something so run faster and when I round the corner, he's there, standing on the balcony.

'Sage? Where the hell have you been? How are you outside? Where is April?' He asks me in rapid concession.

'Outside round the front, no clue and-' I pause, looking at the ground and not wanting to say it. He understands already and doesn't push me for more when I meet his eye.

'I can't get out of the room; the door won't budge. Can you get inside and help me?'

'The thing is…' I explain to him the situation.

'You have got to be *kidding* me.' He hits the rails in frustration. I look at the building to see if there's any way to climb down but there isn't.

'I'll try, Jonas, I will. Hold on-'

'No!' He shouts, holding a hand up at me. 'Don't waste time trying, you're outside and blinking so go get help, find the nearest house and ring the fire brigade.'

'I'm going.'

'Please hur-'

The clock lets out another chime.

I wonder how on earth I can hear it from outside, with the sound of the flames over it too. I feel it ring through my ears so clearly.

I stop and come back. I don't know who the chime is for, all I know is one of us is outside and one is inside. 'Jonas?' I shout up to him and he's still him for now as he's looking around in panic, sweat rolling down from his forehead and wetting his shirt.

'What did I say? What did I say?' He doesn't look at me as he says this, I think he's asking himself.

I already know what he said. I've known for a while. *I'll kill myself.*

I watch him rush back into the room and shove the door. After a minute or so of trying, he runs back out and looks down, trying to find a way down safely as I had done.

He's looking at me, crying. 'I don't want to die.'

I'm too lost for words to say anything. How do you reply to that?

I don't need to.

I watch as his body goes rigid, his hands grasp the rails of the balcony, and he looks down at the ground. 'Jonas?' I whisper as, even if I shouted it, I don't think he would hear me.

He climbs over the edge, his hands still gripping the balcony as he leans forward. I run over to stand where he's leaning over. I can catch him. It'll hurt like hell, but he'll be alive and outside. He lets go of the railing and I brace to catch him, but he falls to the left unexpectedly, like he was pushed that way and hits the ground hard with a crunch and a crack.

I run to him. 'Jonas?' I say carefully. I kneel and move his head slightly to see his glasses have cracked and his eyes open. I check his pulse and can't find any sign of life left in him. I roll him over to try and resuscitate him but when I gently move his face into position, his body suddenly jerks causing me to jump. 'Jonas?'

I watch as he cracks every bone, his arms and legs moving violently on the ground. His mouth drops open and his tongue flops out as his neck turns in a circle, snapping every time it moves a notch. When his head returns to its normal spot, it flops to one side, his spine showing through the back of his head. His arms and legs slow and go rigid, flopping to the ground.

There's nothing I can do.

I turn to see the fire has reached the second floor as I hear one of the windows smash somewhere from around the front. I walk around and look through the kitchen window but not for long as I can feel the heat burn me.

I just stand there and watch my world burn, and the people I knew for a blink go with it.

Chapter 13

I sit there until the fire stops.

It has consumed the whole house during the night and into the early hours of the morning. I couldn't tell you the time, maybe that damn clock could if it was still there.

I was worried it would grow to the fields, but it never surpassed the house. It burnt itself out. Not that I am the expert on fires, but I don't think that's how they work, at least ones like this. It took nearly everything with it, even Reece, Hallie, April, and Jonas are gone. I checked. Can't even bury them, cremation was chosen for them. Even Jonas who wasn't inside, I found a pile of black ash where he had landed.

My life's work is gone too, I try not to focus on that fact, but I'm not known for backups and autosaving. I think about their stories gone too, the start of Reece's sequel, all of Hallie's and Jonas' notes, and April's new story in a new world. It's really not important anymore but as a writer, I can't help but think about it. I don't know how it was for them, but my writing was everything. The only small silver lining is, most of them already had their works out in the world, their stamp, the way people will remember them. It hurts me to think that Hallie doesn't have that, this was going to be her mark on the world.

I waited for it to take me.

I searched my brain for what I had said, what my fate would be. I can't remember anything though. I'm tempted even now to throw out a statement as how could I continue after this? But then I remember Spence and everyone else. It hurts to think how they might feel if I didn't go home. I then think about what it's going to be like for Reece, Hallie, April, and Jonas' families and how on earth I would even tell them what happened. Would they blame me? I would blame me.

I've become the trope I had joked about all this time. I am a final girl.

The house just stands there, whiffs of smoke still lingering around. A desolate place filled with souls, old and now new. Judging by the memories, it could mean they are all trapped here somewhere. I don't even know how to help them rest. Maybe if I still had the book I could but that's gone too, another thing I checked for.

One thing is still clearly standing, the fireplace.

It is still lit but now has a more controlled fire. I stand up and look at it, watching the flames once again wondering when they would ingest me if I got too close.

I wouldn't give it the chance.

I pick up the fire poker and whack it as hard as I can, anything to destroy this monstrosity. I drag the firewood out of the fire as fast as I can but every time I look back, more firewood has replaced it. I yell with frustration and start to tear up, dropping to my knees.

'I wouldn't do that if I were you.'

I turn to see him. I didn't even hear any footsteps but there he stands. 'I guess I should make my apologies to the owner for the state of the house, not that I had any control over it. I better be getting my deposit back, regardless.' I charge over to him with the fire poker at the ready. I point it at him. 'Which one are you?' I can feel my blood boil, saying each word through gritted teeth. 'No more games, I'm tired of them. Truth, give me the truth.'

I expect him to deny it, to keep up the overexcited man persona he had given me just yesterday in the village. 'I was Silas,' he says, with a sense of sadness in his voice.

I had expected Arlo or even Victor over him, but I look at his light hair and know him to not be lying. 'Rosemary succeeded? You died; you came back?' I can't be dealing with the undead as well as the darkness we had already dealt with. He hasn't aged, he would be an old man by now or would have died of old age.

'No, I never really came back.' His voice is soft and low, like a completely different person from yesterday. Yesterday's Silas felt like a child, luring me into a trap.

'You've had some sort of life though. You're still here, walking around.'

'I'm not really here anymore.'

'Yet, here you stand,' I say, my voice getting louder and angrier. 'Your family is all dead. Wasn't it enough that your brother, sister-in-law, and granddaughter died? No, you had to take your great-niece's life too. Lure her here to burn to death. Bet you would have tried for Victor too, the whole set if he was still around.'

'I had no choice-'

'Bullshit.' I sound out both syllables, feeling the spit coming out, the shakiness uncontrollable.

He hangs his head, whether in shame or because he got caught, I can't tell for sure. He lifts his head to look me in the eye. 'I have no control, only a little right now. Only to make the game more fun for them.' He grunts and lets out a yelp in pain, bending over to clutch his stomach. He has said too much. I remember how the owner had helped us in small ways, like suggesting to April to take Rosemary's room, he knew what we would find. 'It is my fault, that those things were summoned and are still here. I'm still dead – I was never bought back to life, just my body as the first part of the deal and part of my soul. Now, I'm stuck like this forever.'

I control myself; I need to know more. 'Because the deal was never completed.'

He nods. 'It didn't matter if it was a stranger's life, she wouldn't sacrifice someone for me or for anyone. So, the demons stayed and well.' He gestures to the ruins of the house. 'You see how they like to play. And they left me like this, a body, a hollow shape most of the time. They've only had me for a long time and that gets boring. You've seen how they do it, they don't hold real power until words are spoken. It's all just a bit of fun for them.'

'Now the deal can never be completed. Or is that why I'm still here? I'm the sacrifice at the end?'

He laughs as he shakes his head, there's no heart in it though. 'They never cared about sealing the deal.' He grunts again in pain, kneeling over to face the ground. 'They don't want to go home; they want to stay and keep eating.'

I gulp. 'Eating?'

'Their souls.' He sees my face. 'I'm so sorry.'

'They've run out of Taylors though.'

'That no longer matters, now they've completed the set. As much as they can at least.' His voice is no longer soft but distorted. He lifts his head and gives me that terrifying smile, that hungry grin. 'They have you.'

Silas' body drops abruptly, the life leaving his eyes and a dark figure emerges from him, lingering over me.

I hear the flames spark behind me and watch as another dark figure crawls out of the fireplace to loom behind me. There is a pencil in one of its hands.

'Well,' their voices say, with a devouring smile 'you asked for a story, we gave you one.'

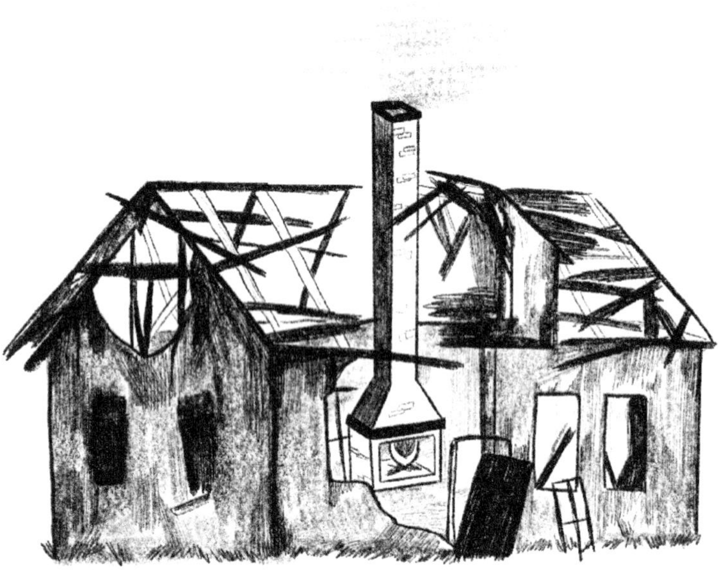

Acknowledgments

I've been writing for many, many, many years so to see this book completed and out in the world is an absolute dream. You may be thinking, hang on a minute, wait, you already have two books out before this. True, but I started writing this before those two, so it'll always feel like the first book.

I want to start by thanking the magazine that rejected this as a 3,000-word short story in December of 2021 - you were completely right; it wasn't a finished story. There was so much more to it, a lot more words and tears in fact.

It took me a while to figure out where the story was going but we got there.

To Alien Buddha Press for working with me and publishing this story. I'm so happy to be able to bring my five writers and their stories to life.

A thank you to my family, as always, for asking about my writing and being horrified when I let them read it.

Thank you to the gang: Brooke, Kira, and Connor. Always the first to read and rave about my stories and help with advice and design ideas. What would I do without you? I would be a mess.

I have to mention my little man, Barney, to who the book is dedicated to. And, in case you are wondering, Freddie has his own book and it's coming…

Thinking back to those times when I would sit at my writing desk at home, and they would sleep right behind the chair which made it impossible to get up. It was a great form of motivation.

I should probably mention at this point, if you don't know, they're my dogs.

Thanks to Christy (Grim Poppy Design) for the awesome book cover as always and Natacha (natadibuja) for the artwork of Rosemary Hollow and Afkar (mc_afkar) for the artwork of my boys (you'll see when you turn the page).

And, to you, for reading this story. Thank you.

Lauren (she/they) is a library assistant by day and writer by night. She is the author of WHEN THE DEMONS TAKE HOLD, YOUR DARLING DEATH, and LET'S ALL GO TO THE LOBBY.

She has several published short stories including: THE CHILDREN OF OWL WILDS with Haunted Words Press, ALIVE, JUST with The Horror Tree, and THE SACRIFICES WE MAKE with Rooster Republic Press.

Printed in Great Britain
by Amazon